D0849845

SEVEN

OF

INFINITIES

Aliette de Bodard

Subterranean Press

2020

Edited by Yanni Kuznia

First Edition

ISBN
978-1-59606-976-3

Subterranean Press
PO Box 190106
Burton, MI 48519

subterraneanpress.com

Manufactured in the United States of America

IGH-RANKING VISITOR in the antechamber, *waiting for you.*

When her bots pinged her unexpectedly with that message, Vân opened the door of her room, and found the mindship *The Wild Orchid in Sunless Woods* in the narrow space that served as common access to the quarters she and her student Uyên occupied.

What was the mindship doing there?

She was a member of Vân's poetry club, except that she was a mindship and a celebrated scholar who'd graduated from the imperial examinations—whereas Vân was the daughter of a shopkeeper, with no degree to her name, making ends meet as a private tutor rather than enjoying the largesse of being a state official. *Sunless Woods* and Vân spent time together in the context of the poetry club, but certainly they'd never been intimate enough for the ship to pay her a private call.

Vân stepped into the antechamber. "Elder aunt. Are you here for me?"

"Child." The ship rose, and bowed. "Yes, I am." She wasn't physically there: she was parked in orbit somewhere in the Scattered Pearls Belt, projecting down an avatar when she needed to be in the habitats. Her avatar was as unconventional as her name (which was itself a reference to scholars whose merit wasn't recognised, a borderline criticism of the examinations system). Instead of a miniature version of herself, it was a vaguely humanoid shape: at first glance, she appeared to have two arms and two legs and to be about Vân's size, but whenever she moved Vân would catch a glimpse of something far, far larger—sleek and polished metal, the reflection of distant stars, and a feeling the room, the entire habitat were twisting and folding back on themselves, unable to contain the vastness of her.

"Is there a place we could talk privately?" Vân couldn't place *Sunless Woods*'s tone.

"Yes, of course." She led *Sunless Woods* back into her compartment: her own private space, a small room with a bed, a table and a series of overlays of paintings and ceramics whose physical version Vân could certainly never have afforded. "Do you want tea?"

"Please." The ship inclined her head.

The bots poured Vân a cup of tea—and a ghostly cup shimmered into existence for *Sunless Woods*, in an overlay of Vân's room. The mindship didn't need food to sustain her body, but to her the complex, layered flavour of the tea would suggest pleasant memories—the same for Vân, reminding her of New Year's Eve and the smell of banana leaves, and the crinkle of red envelopes handed to children.

The ship waited until Vân was almost done with her cup of tea before speaking. "I came here because there have been… discussions."

"Discussions?"

Sunless Woods's tone was dark. "On the suitability of your presence at the poetry club."

For a moment—a suspended, agonising, horrible moment—Vân thought they had found her out. That they knew about Laureate An Thành, that the scandal she'd been running away from had finally caught her.

How could they know? Laureate An Thành said, in Vân's mind. *They can't possibly tell the difference.* Her voice was withering. Vân could feel An Thành in her thoughts—a personality on a mem-implant offering Vân the knowledge she needed to go from passably good scholar to an excellent one. Mem-implants were commonplace, but they were ancestors of those who held them, physical people preserved as study-aids—and An Thành, whom Vân had put together from fragments of other people's personalities, was the height of impropriety, disrespectfully scavenged from the dead and not related to Vân in any way.

They— Vân struggled for words amidst the bottomless pit in her stomach, and saw *Sunless Woods*, head cocked, watching her. "Elder aunt—"

The ship shrugged. It was a curiously expansive gesture that seemed to drag the air away from Vân. Her voice was dark. "They think you commonplace. Vulgar."

Vulgar. Vân stared at her: this was familiar territory. Her heart sank. "This isn't about my ability as a scholar at all, is it?"

For a moment she thought the ship would smile and lie, but *Sunless Woods* merely shook her head, her face taking on the hard planes of some faceted gem. "This is about your birth." She smiled, but it was darker and a great deal less amused than Vân would have thought. "They use words like unsuitable, brash, unaware of the codes by which they all live."

Because she hadn't grown up with these codes. Laureate An Thành could help, to an extent—could offer knowledge and literary allusions, but of course something would always seem off to the other scholars, the ones whose families had been officials for generations. Vân said, chilled, "If the poetry club throws me out, I'll lose my job."

Word would get around. Uyên, her student, the daughter of the house in which Vân lived, wouldn't want a tutor who was shunned by the scholar community.

Vân would lose everything.

Sunless Woods said, "I know." It was rather sharper than Vân had expected.

"I don't understand why you're here," Vân said.

A ping, on the network: someone else had entered the antechamber. A woman Vân didn't know: middle-aged, her skin shining with the particular smoothness of cheap rejuv treatments. She wore only a handful of bots, like jewellery rather than the usual utilitarian approach: three serpentine ones wrapped around both wrists and around her neck—the lacquered, ornamental kind painted with vivid orchids. Vân couldn't place her socially, which was odd because she usually had an excellent sense of where people fitted in on the habitats. "Hang on," she said, half-rising.

But the door to the other compartment—Uyên's compartment—had already opened, and Vân's student Uyên stepped out. "Oh hello, younger aunt. Do come in."

And they were both gone into Uyên's compartment. Vân breathed out. None of her business, then.

Good.

"Why am I here?" *Sunless Woods* said. "To warn you."

Vân opened her mouth. That was not the answer she had expected. "You can't possibly—?"

"Disapprove of what they're doing?" *Sunless Woods*'s voice was sharp. "This is about merit, not about who your parents were."

As if that had ever been the case. Vân said, trying to breathe through the panic—what would she do, if Uyên's family dismissed her?—"I don't know what to do."

"Appeal," *Sunless Woods*'s voice was sharp. "Good steeds don't always get the proper grooms, or jade the right carver to make it come alive." *Metaphors for scholars whose talents were going unrecognised*, An Thành pointed out in Vân's thoughts. *The last one is a bit unorthodox.*

"I—" Vân opened her mouth, closed it. She couldn't appeal. She couldn't afford to appeal. A board would take a look at her scholarly abilities, and if they dug too deep they'd find that Vân couldn't possibly have a real mem-implant—and the scandal that followed would be even larger and uglier. It would lose her her job anyway, and see her shunned from good society forever. "I can't, elder aunt."

"Can't, or won't?" *Sunless Woods*'s gaze held Vân's, unerringly: in the faint imprint of pupils on the ship's face Vân saw darkness, an exhilarating and endless plunge into the stars. She shivered.

Either. Both. "If I force the poetry club to keep me on, you know they'll just resent me for who I am." She tried, very hard, to make it seem reasonable, to not show *Sunless Woods* an inkling of fear.

A snort. "You can live with resentment." The ship cocked her head to watch her. "Or would you rather lose your job?"

"I don't understand why you're here," Vân said, again, stubbornly.

"Because things should be fair. Because you're talented, and because this would be a colossal, infuriating waste."

"I'm not—" Vân started, but a voice cut her off.

"Teacher?" Startled, Vân looked up. Her student Uyên was standing in the doorway, and something was off in her pose.

"What's wrong?"

"I—" Uyên stopped, spoke up again. Her voice was shaking. "I think I have a problem."

"What kind of problem?"

"My visitor. She's dead," Uyên said, and raised hands that were shaking—and would have collapsed, if Vân hadn't leapt from her chair to catch her as she faltered.

UYÊN'S CURRENT OVERLAY of her compartment was darkness: a vast and cavernous view of the heavens as if one were in a spaceship or small capsule, and the floor were glass. Beneath Vân's feet was the River of Stars: a spread of lights underfoot that kept changing, drawing patterns that evoked words—fragments of poems by Hàn Mặc Tử, Lãnh Ngọc, Đông Hải Diễm…

Beautiful, Laureate An Thành said. *Uyên is such a very promising student. No wonder her mother has such high hopes for her. The daughter of the Captain who Swam in the River of Stars…*

Vân shook her head to dismiss the comments. Now wasn't the time to let the Laureate take over. *Literature later. There's a body, Laureate.*

An Thành subsided, with a regretful sigh, and sank to a bare whisper in Vân's mind again.

The woman Vân had seen earlier lay on one of those ever-shifting spreads of stars, her face by turns in light and shadow as the composition beneath her changed. Vân couldn't see any wounds.

"May I?" *Sunless Woods* had followed her in.

Vân wasn't sure if she was addressing Vân or Uyên; but Uyên hadn't moved; was waiting for her to weigh in as the most senior person in the room. She nodded.

Sunless Woods moved, graceful, ethereal. Vân blinked, and all of a sudden *Sunless Woods* was no longer in the doorway, but kneeling by the corpse's side, head cocked to stare at it, fingers resting lightly on the woman's wrists, where her bots still lay coiled. Something spun in the air between them: a thread of light going from one to another, as *Sunless Woods* tipped her head back, lips parted—she seemed to be inhaling it all.

"What happened?" Vân asked.

"I don't know," Uyên said, and Vân measured the depth of her student's panic. Uyên would rather deflect conversation than admit ignorance. "She said she had important business. I left her in there thirty seconds to rustle up some cooking bots for tea and refreshments, and when I came back she was on the floor. She had no pulse!"

Vân raised a hand, trying to stem Uyên's panic. She was wound up too tight, still worrying about the poetry club and all that it might entail for her. She was meant to project reassurance, but she felt small and scared and vulnerable. She forced herself to breathe. "All right. Back up. What happened before that? Who was she?"

Uyên made a face. "I don't know."

"What do you mean, you don't know? You—" Vân breathed in, again, slowing down. She wanted to say Uyên had been so effortlessly certain when she'd welcomed the woman in, but then she realised that Uyên would never look uncertain. She was so deeply worried of being judged and found wanting that her mask had become second nature to her. "So you didn't know her?"

"No," Uyên said. "She said she had some urgent business, and that it had to do with the examinations."

The ones Uyên was meant to be sitting for in a couple of months—the ones Vân had been hired to help her pass, to make Uyên worthy of the first mother who had died for the Empire and given Uyên and her second mother the grace of an imperial title. "With the examinations?" Vân frowned. "Surely she'd know better than selling questions or cheating methods. The law is quite drastic on the matter."

The only things allowed in the candidates' cells during the examinations would be mem-implants—like the one Vân had, like the two Uyên had, the memory traces of her first mother and grandmother, offering advice and suggestions, the ancestors' blessings made manifest.

Sunless Woods shifted. "You're aware," she said to Uyên, "that if she'd been found guilty of examination fraud you'd have been judged guilty as well." She brought her fingers from the corpse's wrist to her mouth, held them there for a while, as if pondering a particularly difficult problem.

An expansive shrug from Uyên. "I know the code. If I haven't accepted anything then there's no offence."

Sunless Woods took the fingers out of her mouth. "You'd need to prove it. Jurisprudence isn't on your side. It's a really odd corpse." She shifted—her eyes rolled up for a moment, and in that fraction of a heartbeat Vân saw the deepness of space in them, like a gateway to a place that would swallow her whole. "There's no pulse, but there's also no wounds whatsoever. Burn marks on her hands, but these aren't lethal, and they're also a few days old, at the least."

"Poison?" Uyên asked.

Focus. Focus. She needed to think less on herself and more about her student, or she was going to fail Uyên. "Look, none of it is the point. The point is that we need to call the militia and let them handle this, to get you off the hook. Now."

Uyên looked puzzled.

"Examination fraud is bad enough. Murder is worse," Vân said.

If she closed her eyes she'd see the interrogation rooms again; the officious looking clerk smiling at her and gently, carefully insinuating that she knew more than she let on about

the affairs of her friends—that surely one had to be spectacularly stupid, or unaware, or a poor elder sister, to fail to see what
was right in front of her eyes—and Vân, remaining silent and
not knowing what she could do…

It was past. She had survived, but Hương Lâm and Dinh had
not. She remembered the day both sisters had been transferred
to the Twenty-Third Planet for their execution—standing in
the crowd of the spaceport, trying to catch a glimpse of them,
and Hương Lâm's gaze finding her as the militia pushed her
towards the transport mindship—the way her friend's face had
set, lips tightening, the little shake of her head that warned Vân
no to do anything stupid.

We protected you, big'sis. Don't go and waste it all.

It was in the past. Five years ago, and all that remained of it
was dark and confused nightmares in which she never ran fast
enough to escape.

A touch, on Vân's shoulders—a warmth that was too sudden and too spread to be that of a human hand, but rather
something processed through an overlay. She looked up. *Sunless
Woods* had effortlessly crossed the room and was standing by
her side—and behind her, along her trajectory, was a faint
imprint on Uyên's overlay, like the radiance of ten thousand
stars fading against the daylight sky. "Can I have a word with
you, child? In private."

Vân clamped her lips on the obvious "why?" that filled her
thoughts. "Of course."

She walked with *Sunless Woods* to a quieter corner of the room. A hush descended: the mindship, accessing the habitat's command and asking for privacy. "I didn't know you could do that."

A smile that transformed *Sunless Woods*'s entire face, making her seem less distant and less severe. "Technically, no. But I have ways."

"All right," Vân said. "What do you want?"

Sunless Woods's face was gentle. "Are you all right? You looked upset."

Vân's lips moved before her brain caught up with them. "Why do you care?"

A fraught silence. *Sunless Woods* moved to put a hand on Vân's shoulder again. When she raised her arm oily darkness glinted in the space between arm and torso, as if she were trailing a cape of the cloth of Heaven—an unsettling and yet oddly welcome sight, a reminder that all of Vân's concerns were, in the end, short-lived. Warmth spread, again, diffuse and unoppressive. She'd never craved anything so much.

"I'm sorry." *Sunless Woods* withdrew her hand—Vân found herself following it with her eyes, and had to bodily stop herself from trying to grab it and pull it back towards her. Pointless: it would have taken a shift of overlays and specific instructions before she could actually interact with *Sunless Woods*. "I shouldn't have touched you without your permission," *Sunless Woods* said.

"No, it's all right," Vân said. And, forcing herself to find words in the desert of her thoughts—for a brief moment nothing came, and then Laureate An Thành was there, offering poems and references on friendship and loss and desire.

As my ship tears itself from orbit
My heart twists and turns with the stars
Pained, falling and falling,
As I remember butterflies flitting from orchid to orchid…

Not helpful, Vân snapped. She certainly wasn't going to sleep with *Sunless Woods*. The thought she ever would was ridiculous. They moved in such different circles it would be short, awkward, and just create more resentment than pleasure. "It's all right. I'm sorry I snapped at you." And then, before she could stop herself, "I liked it."

"Ah." Again, a pregnant silence that stretched until it felt it would snap.

Vân said, "I had a bad experience with the militia when I was much younger." An exhaled breath. She couldn't get Hương Lâm's pale face out of her head. "It's all right." She raised a hand to forestall *Sunless Woods's* objections. "I was just a witness to a brawl. But that's why I know how bad they can get, even with innocents." Not a lie, but not the whole truth, either.

"Hmmm." *Sunless Woods* cocked her head, watching her for a while. Weighing her—except that this time it wasn't about whether she thought Vân worthy, but something else entirely. Taking in the whole of her and…

Her mind blanked. She was afraid to ask a question that she knew *Sunless Woods* would answer with the same cool, devastating honesty.

At length, *Sunless Woods* said, with unexpected sharpness in her voice, "They're unfeeling louts drunk on their own power, and you should never have had to deal with any of that. Will you give me permission?"

"For what?"

Vân thought it would be about touching again—about what would come afterwards, a host of confused feelings within her suddenly clamouring for nebulous release—but *Sunless Woods* merely said, "I would like to, ah. Involve myself in this."

Vân tried—and failed—to slow down the heartbeat that seemed to be resonating all the way into her fingers. "You? Elder aunt…"

"I can stand between you and the militia. You'd find dealing with them difficult."

"Not as much as Uyên would. I have no intention of shirking my duties." She'd clamped down on the other panic, the fear she'd lose the poetry club and her livelihood: this was more urgent and the consequences would be far more drastic.

Fond, amused laughter from the ship, coming back to her in trailing echoes that bore no resemblance to the geometry of the room. "Of course you don't. Nevertheless… The other thing is that I'd want to look into this myself."

"Surely the militia—"

"Oh, never fear, we'll call them. But you know as well as I do that this is a single-tribunal posting, outside of the numbered planets. The militia is overworked; the magistrate young, inexperienced and flooded with requests."

"I don't understand," Vân said. "You're a scholar."

A silence, stretching for just slightly longer than it should. When *Sunless Woods* spoke again, she said, "And as a scholar, I'm curious about anything that would affect the examinations," but Vân had the distinct feeling the answer would have been quite different if the mindship hadn't checked herself. "And I'm not without resources of my own."

Vân had never been good at diplomacy: her old childhood dream of being a scholar in the imperial palace had been as unrealistic as it had been high-flown. "Fine. If you tell me why. Really why."

That same laughter, startling her with how utterly young and carefree it sounded. The mindship was ancient. She had to be: mindships all were, and in the club's meetings she'd made it clear she'd already been an adult at the time of the uprising, seven years ago. "I'm curious," *Sunless Woods* said, finally. Noise came rushing back in, and she walked back to the corpse, gesturing for Vân to follow her. She lifted one arm, so that the elaborate and overlarge silk sleeves fell down, baring its length. "Here."

At first, all Vân saw was skin, brown and paler than her own, and with the faintest hint of the particular tan that came from too much time spent in space. But then something shifted: layers of disguises peeling away like a cook expertly slicing at meat, until an archaic symbol shone, visible across all the overlays—the way it should always have been, a mark that couldn't be disguised or removed for anyone with the right query tools.

"Furtive theft," Vân said, aloud. And, on the other arm, the same symbol. Not only a thief with an offence grave enough to be marked, but a recidivist. "Child?"

"I told you, I don't know her!" Uyên said.

Vân didn't think she was lying.

Sunless Woods didn't seem to, either: her whole attention was on the corpse. "It's a good disguise," she said. "A very expensive one: they're not temporary mods. She's altered her whole being, including genetic modifications. Finding out who she originally was is going to be extremely difficult if not outright impossible. Which means that whatever else she was, she wasn't poor, or without means. And whatever she wanted from Uyên, it had to be worth all this."

Vân said, stubbornly, "I still don't see why—"

"I'm involved?" *Sunless Woods* stood up in a fluid movement, her head turning thoughtfully taking in the entire room. The effect was uncanny. "Call it…a challenge."

THE WILD ORCHID in *Sunless Woods* was old, and experienced, and she really, really shouldn't have involved herself. For starters, *Sunless Woods* wasn't her real name, and contrary to what she'd told Vân, she wasn't really a scholar, either; or native to the Scattered Pearls Belt, or a decorated hero of the uprising. Just like the dead woman, *Sunless Woods* was a thief; and she supposed that the only thing that separated her from the corpse was that she'd never been caught. Throughout the years, she'd carried a succession of identities and names, slipping in and out of them as easily as a human would put on new clothes. She'd lied and stolen and laughed her way through the Đại Việt empire; and come here in the Belt…well, for a rest, she supposed. For a chance to enjoy life rather than test herself, again and again, against the rocks of the world. The last thing she should have done was involve herself with the affairs of the militia, or give them any reason to question her identity.

And yet…and yet, she liked Vân.

Most of the scholars she'd met were puffed up with their own importance, or utterly certain of the way the world was made—with them at the apex as their natural, Heaven-given right. Vân was the kind of person who walked through the world expecting it to kick her: even her reaction to the poetry club trying to dismiss her had been typical—fear, not the outrage *Sunless Woods* had felt on her behalf. She was currently standing next to *Sunless Woods* and trying very hard not to show how nervous she was.

"I don't understand," Vân said, staring at the compartment in front of them. The door was narrow but high, metal engraved with an interlocking pattern of lotus flowers and boats. The sign was engraved as well, and with no further decorations in overlay. "Bare-house."

Sunless Woods said, "I have a friend who could help us."

"In here?" Vân's face puckered, close to panic. "It's a—"

Sunless Woods laughed. She couldn't help herself. "My friend has peculiar habits. She doesn't bite, I swear. But she's seen enough dead bodies, and I want to run our little problem by her." It was probably better to leave off said friend's more unsavoury activities, or the exact context in which she'd viewed bodies.

Vân looked as though she'd rather be running the other way. Then her face set. "Uyên risks trouble with the militia if we don't solve this fast."

"Not only with the militia," *Sunless Woods* said. She kept her voice light, inconsequential; because she was worried and didn't want to show it. "Possibly with the murderer. And also... that woman may not have worked alone, and her accomplices will want revenge for her death."

Vân stared at her, for a while. Her usual good-natured face narrowed, became as sharp and as incandescent as a just-forged blade, and *Sunless Woods* suddenly had the uncomfortable feeling that Vân saw through her—not only her motivations for helping Vân, but also everything that she kept a secret.

Something lurched within her—not within her avatar, but within the large metal body in orbit, a gigantic heartbeat in corridors and state rooms suddenly blurring and skipping.

"Serious trouble, then," Vân said. "And you're not the kind of person to exaggerate."

She was. She'd been, depending on her persona. She opened her mouth to protest, and then saw Vân's determined expression. "No," she said, the lie tasting sharp and acrid on her mouth. "I guess not."

Vân squared her shoulders. "Uyên is my student. I hate those places—they're the height of indecency—but that's of no consequence."

A silence. They stared at each other. *Sunless Woods* ached to hug Vân, and knew she couldn't afford to. "It does you credit. Come on, child. It's that way."

The door opened on a narrow corridor, and then a quick succession of five other doors. The second one had the same pattern of lotus flowers and boats as the first one, except that the rightmost part of it was bare, and then on every subsequent door the pattern would be a little smaller, and the emptiness a little larger—until the last door, which had no engravings whatsoever on it: just a sheet of matte metal which reflected only the faintest of silhouettes, like a mirror that had lost its silvering. The darkness was absolute.

Behind the last door was a counter, where a bored-looking employee handed them tokens in the same kind of metal as the last door. He did a double-take when he saw *Sunless Woods*, and put back the token he had been about to give her, to retrieve another one from the pile—not a physical one but a thing that existed only in overlay. "Here. You know the rules."

Vân was already disrobing, with visible discomfort. Her bots piled up, inert, on the pile of clothes: the token she was wearing would disconnect her from the habitat's network and prevent the display of any overlays.

Sunless Woods's token tingled in the palm of her hand. The sensation of coldness spread from there to the rest of her body, a tightness that seemed to be getting worse and worse until she felt curiously weightless and empty: the sensation of her own metal body in orbit, which was always running in the background, had been temporarily…not removed, because it would have been impossible for her avatar to exist, but attenuated so much that it might as well be.

Truth was, she hated the bare-house as much as Vân, but for different reasons. She wasn't even sure she understood why *The Bearer of Healing Wine* chose to spend their habitat-bound days there.

"Let's go," she said.

Most people who came to the bare-house came there for calm: to remember the bodies they were rooted in without layers of clothes and overlays, or the distraction of the network. An unpleasant enough experience for a human; a borderline torture for a mindship, whose ability to interact with people not onboard their bodies happened through bots and avatars. Silence was not required, but it was often respected. *Sunless Woods* and Vân wove their way through room after room—people reclining in seats, or sitting at tables and sipping tea laced with hallucinogenics, making quiet conversation or drunken poetry—a handful of naked scholars feverishly committing their latest creations to memory, or to the mercy of fragile and irreplaceable paper.

Vân was turning betel-nut-red after the third such room. "These are—"

"The foremost poets of the Belt?" *Sunless Woods* laughed. She'd had her share of lovers, shipminds and humans both; and she did like Vân but wasn't attracted to her. Or at least shouldn't have been; but for a brief moment as Vân turned towards her, she saw the taut way Vân held herself—and longed to run a cascade of bots down her spine until that tautness became something else—a tight breathless desire that would make Vân feel, if only for a single moment, that she was free. "Some of them. It does give you a different perspective, doesn't it?"

Vân's face was answer enough. *Sunless Woods* let her hand brush Vân's shoulder, though Vân wouldn't be able to feel anything. "Come on. She's over there."

They found *The Bearer of Healing Wine* at the back of the bare-house, sitting in a room without windows or decoration. Her avatar was the classic one of a ship: a smaller version of the sleek, spiked shape that would be in orbit around the belt. She was staring, intently, at the shape of a splayed-out bot on the table: it had been neatly taken apart with every component set a little apart from its neighbours.

"Attempting to understand the secrets of the universe again?" *Sunless Woods* asked.

Wine shifted, moving so that her avatar faced *Sunless Woods;* though in reality it was a shifting of attention more than that of meaningless physical manifestation. "Ah, elder aunt. Didn't expect to see you quite so soon. The house was kind enough to lend me this."

Without bots, she wouldn't have been able to take it apart; and with only a fragmentary network she couldn't even enjoy tea or food or any of the other overlay delicacies. But it pleased her, for some reason. "I still don't understand why you like it so much," *Sunless Woods* said. *Wine* was—had been her lookout: the one who made the maps of the places they'd steal from, and stood watch. She could move through corridors lightning-fast, if needed. And, as a backup, like *Sunless Woods*, she could serve as a getaway ship. They'd seldom had to use that option, because things hadn't gone that badly wrong.

A silence, like a human shrug. "It's...relaxing. Like deep spaces, but without being accountable to any passengers or official or traffic harmony. Oh." She turned. "Forgive me, I hadn't seen you brought a friend."

Vân had been carefully gauging the interplay between both ships: because when she bowed, it was with the politeness applicable to a slightly older peer. "Elder aunt."

Laughter. "Big'sis will do. Where do you keep finding them?"

"We're in the same poetry club," Vân said, blushing again. It was adorable. "She said you could help."

"Help?" *Wine* sounded puzzled, and a little sarcastic.

Sunless Woods said, "We have a mysterious corpse."

The other ship's laughter made the room shake. "Always these, isn't it?"

Sunless Woods gave her a warning, edged smile.

"Ah," *Wine* said, understanding without words the issue—that Vân didn't know who *Sunless Woods* was. "One of these. What about the corpse?"

Sunless Woods rubbed at the token in the palm of her hand, the one that confined her to a single, small, localised body. "It would be much faster if I could share sensory input with you."

"Well, tough luck," *Wine* said. "Try words. Last I recalled, you were pretty glib."

Sunless Woods was no scholar, but she loved words—because they were the pathways to humans and shipminds alike—because she had her avatar and her bots, but neither of them had as much impact as the hooks words could dig in people's brains—to flatter, to seduce, to incense. But her current persona wasn't glib or silver-tongued, and of course *Wine* knew who she really was, but Vân didn't.

Sunless Woods summarised, as best as she could, the state of the body as she'd found it. "Branded thief," she concluded with. "And—I thought she'd been poisoned, but I don't think the symptoms match, so I want your opinion."

"Hmmmm."

"I scanned the body." *Sunless Woods* ignored Vân's look of shock. "Every organ was collapsing at the same time. She must have been in excruciating pain, if only for a short while. I'd have said tortured, but—"

"Yes, that's usually matched by physical wounds. *Khi*-flow in the body?"

"Bad. Not completely blocked out, but starved in all the meridians."

"Mmm. The eyes, what about them? What colour were the whites?"

If *Sunless Woods* had had access to her records, that would have been a much easier question.

It was Vân who spoke up, looking clearly ill at ease. "Something was off with her eyes. I thought she might have been smoking Hell Bridge or Lantern Poppy, but…"

"Tinged with grey, then." *Wine* snorted, very gently. "That's very unusual, but I've definitely seen it before. It wouldn't be surprising, if she was a branded thief. Death by exile implants."

"I was afraid of that," *Sunless Woods* said. "Do you know—"

"Who she was? No," *Wine* said. "Your thief was condemned to exile, and the perimeter of this exile didn't include the Scattered Pearls Belt. But she came back anyway, and the implants the tribunal injected her with ate her alive—as a warning to get out, and then as a punishment when she didn't."

A silence. Vân had looked shocked, now she was horrified. "She didn't look—"

"Like she was in pain?" *Wine* laughed. "Some people are very good at hiding it."

"Mmmm." *Sunless Woods* liked this less and less. Uyên had inherited a compassion title by virtue of her dead mother, but her family, the Lotus Vũ, were small and rather insignificant. Yes, Uyên herself was promising and brilliant, but her surviving mother had barely any money to pay Vân's salary. If *Sunless Woods* had still been at her old occupation—if she hadn't retired or taken a break or whatever she was currently doing—she would only have visited the habitat of the Lotus Vũ if she had a very good reason. A love affair, or a heist that needed to be cased beforehand.

Uyên hadn't known the woman, and anyway wouldn't have been attracted to that type. So not a love affair. A heist, then—except that this was the kind of heist that had led an exile in terrible pain to return to a place that would kill her. *Sunless Woods* said, aloud, "She must have wanted something very, very badly."

"Hmmm." *Wine* was pensive. She said, at last, "That kind of bad never ends well."

"You mean she's dead," Vân said. "Surely—"

"Surely she wasn't working alone," *Sunless Woods* said, more sharply than she'd intended to. Her own old crew had scattered—except for *Wine*, and a few others who still owed her favours or loyalty or both—but a theft, even in this kind of place, would have taken, oh, a bare minimum of three or four people. "And something like that, wanted badly enough? I don't think death, or the militia, will stop the rest of them."

"I agree," *Wine* said.

"But—" Vân started, checked herself. "Why Uyên?"

"I don't know," *Sunless Woods* said, with some irritation. She'd hoped to impress and comfort Vân, and obviously it had just opened more questions. She'd sent the remnants of her crew digging what they could on Uyên, too; but so far they'd come up empty-handed. Uyên liked drinking and going out with other candidates at night, and didn't always show up at her lessons with enough sleep, though she always made an effort to be punctual. But that hardly set her apart from literally any other teenager in the Belt.

Vân's face set again. "Well, that won't do. My thanks, big-'sis," she said to *Wine*. And she turned on her heel and was halfway gone from the room before *Sunless Wood* found words.

"Wait. Where are you going?"

"To give Uyên a stern talking-to until she discloses whatever she's been hiding from me," Vân said. "What else?"

There was silence, for a while, after Vân left. *Wine* broke it. "Your latest interest?" she asked.

"I'm retired," *Sunless Woods* said, more irritated than she should have been.

"From thieving, or loving, or both?"

"I'm not answering that."

A snort from *Wine.* "Of course you wouldn't. And admit it—you're bored."

Sunless Woods said nothing for a while. She knelt by the table, and stared at the splayed-out bot. Metal legs, and optical bands, and here, the processing unit that would relay simple orders through the network... "What about you? Are you retired as well? Back to commercial transport, for the good of the Empire..."

"You know what I think of the empire," *Wine* snapped. And, in a softer tone, "But you also know yourself. Obscurity never really suited you. I'm surprised you've held out as long. A year?"

"A year is nothing in shipminds' lifespans," *Sunless Woods* said. But...but, nevertheless, she was no longer making headlines. No more holos or vids of her thefts or the daring escapes—no news channels running her scathing memorials against the order of things. Instead, she was a member of a poetry club—a good, law-abiding member of society, upholding the order of things.

Wine wasn't speaking. *Sunless Woods* would have asked her why she enjoyed it so much here, but she knew the answer already: that in the bare-house, *Wine* wasn't beholden to anyone or anything—no duties or bonds or endless demands on her from a society she'd gladly set afire. "You're right," *Sunless Woods* said. "It's so dreadfully boring, being an honest ship."

"Investigating a murder is practically militia work," *Wine* said.

"You've seen Vân. You know the militia will eat her alive."

"Oh, I have," *Wine* said. "I like her. She's got that same fire burning that we all did once, doesn't she? But not the same taste for the limelight. I wonder if she has your taste for challenges."

Challenges. The thrill of evading guards without ever spilling blood—those tense moments, struggling to hack into a security system, where everything hung in the balance and *Sunless Woods*'s entire life could be upended—and afterwards, seeing her exploits splashed on every news channel—knowing that she was out there, that her name was out there, that people would *know* her and who she was.

But people were fickle, weren't they? And she was very much yesterday's news.

She hadn't expected it to viscerally matter quite as much.

Wine said, finally, "You know we'd come, if you called. The old crew didn't scatter that far. A good ambitious project…"

"We've got all we need," *Sunless Woods* said. "And it was getting too dangerous."

"But—as you said yourself—it was never about money."

"Hmmm." *Sunless Woods* was tempted, in spite of herself—if only to get back at the militia in the Belt, which had so obviously made Vân's life a misery—something large and loud that would show them who truly held the best game tiles. "I'll sort this one out first. That should make enough headlines, shouldn't it?"

"Of course," *Wine* said, in that tone of voice which suggested that she knew exactly how it would turn out.

VÂN MARCHED INTO Uyên's quarters burning with righteous anger—all of which, unfortunately, didn't last past seeing Uyên herself.

The overlay had been switched off, revealing the small cramped room for what it really was—without the mods to increase the sense of walked distance, it was nothing more than a compartment onboard the station, not particularly large or particularly luxurious: a mark of how the grace of Uyên's dead captain mother had only carried them so far. Drawings of various classical figures adorned its walls: brush, ink, paper and ink stone, and images of scholars aboard spaceships, lifting wine cups to the stars.

Uyên herself was sitting at the table where she usually worked on the classics—she had a small overlay open in front of her, a diagram of linked poems and memorials quotes that Vân could recognise but not make sense of. Laureate An Thành came to the fore of Vân's thoughts. *They're just disjointed quotes, no meaning or coherence to them.* Uyên was adding names as Vân came in: not any references that An Thành recognised.

Uyên looked up, and smiled despondently. "Just trying to remember everyone who might have a grudge against us. It's not a really large list."

Something fluttered and broke in Vân's chest. "Child…"

Uyên shrugged—looked at Vân for a moment, and then her usual arrogant mask was back on. "The militia made a mess of things, looking for evidence." She gestured: at first Vân couldn't see anything, but then Laureate An Thành, who had a better eye for detail, pointed out the dents in the metal walls, and the lopsided way some of the house bots walked. "Never mind. I'll make another overlay. A better one. I always thought the poetry was insufficient."

A pause. Clearly a query directed at Vân, who, caught off-guard, floundered, desperately looking for an answer—An Thành puzzled, thinking that the poetry had been in good taste, but obviously Vân had never conceived An Thành to finely analyse feelings of hurt and low self-worth. An Thành was knowledgeable and authoritative, bringing Vân the knowledge she lacked to function in literary circles, the deep-seated, intuitive mastery of the classics that required private tutors and expensive schools, all the chances Vân and her friends at the poorly-funded state school had never had: an act of fundamental redress. *Not the time, Laureate,* Vân said. And, to Uyên, "Everything can be fixed."

The militia. The woman's possible accomplices, looking for revenge. Vân wasn't even sure where she'd start to fix it all, but her duty was to protect Uyên.

"Can the dead walk the station again?" Uyên's voice was bitter.

There is no birth or death, no ebbing or arising. Vân ignored An Thành, and slid next to Uyên on the bench. "Why don't you show me your list?"

It was short, and unfruitful. Uyên's dead mother hadn't had time to make enemies: her rank of captain had been bestowed posthumously, and about the only people who might have held a grudge were the Rợ, the barbarians she had so thoroughly defeated by leaping into the vacuum without the protection of a shadow-suit. Uyên's other mother had a life that *Sunless Woods* would have described as boring: she ran a publishing house which produced scholars' poetry books—the old-fashioned paper kind, as well as full-on sensory immersion ones with custom overlays. As to Uyên herself…

Vân ran down the list of Uyên's possible enemies, trying to contain growing disbelief. "A friend you argued with about the colour of the flowers in Đông Hải Diễm's 'Conduct of Scholars'?"

"We were drunk," Uyên said, with some of her old haughtiness back.

"I see." Vân kept her composure, which was hard to do—both watching Uyên's face, and because Laureate An Thành was keeping up a helpful commentary of which colour the flowers really had been—which managed to combine masterful scholarship and utter uselessness. "Well, it's unlikely any of your arguments with your friends would lead to this." She paused, glanced at the list. A debt owed to another student—but no, it had been a string of coppers, barely enough money to buy a plate of dumplings at the local teahouse. Definitely not the sort of thing that would convince an exiled thief to go die here. "All right, so it's not you." Her gaze wandered around the small, bare room. "But maybe it's this place."

"This place? Really?" Uyên looked sceptical.

Vân couldn't say she was feeling very confident, either. She called up the network, and sent queries about the previous owners of the house. "When did you move in?"

Uyên bit her lip. "The year First Mother received her grace. Ten years ago." Her voice shook: it was barely perceptible.

"I'm sorry," Vân said, in the silence.

Uyên's face was set. "Don't be. I loved her very much, but it was her choice, in the end. She laid down her life to win a battle, and we, in return, were bestowed the imperial grace." She sounded like she was repeating something she'd been told, over and over.

Vân wanted to hug her, except that Uyên was a teenager and her student—if she would even remain that once she found out about the poetry club, but that was an unfair worry to lay at Uyên's feet. Instead Vân said, "Grief is like the bamboo in winter: it never truly dies." It was trite and facile, not the subtle quotes she could have had, if she'd waited for An Thành to weigh in with her own knowledge. But it would have been unfair to Uyên: it was the sentiment that mattered, and this had to come from Vân herself. "You loved her very much, and it does you credit."

Uyên threw a glance at the altar in a corner of the room, with its five tangerines and smouldering stick of incense. The holo on it was her mother, frozen in that everlasting land of youth cut off by death, with the captain's badge she'd never worn in real life. "Filial piety. There's nothing particularly noteworthy about this."

"You know as much as I do that it can become a hollow, facile thing with no love or respect," Vân said. "A performance more than a feeling." She put all the authority she'd gained as a teacher into her words. "A mask over rotten insides."

Uyên said nothing for a while. She laughed, a short and joyless thing. "The only thing I'll ever hide with a mask is what society doesn't want to see."

Namely, how ruthless and dangerous she could be. One of her mothers had looked at approaching enemy vessels, coldly weighed odds and thrown herself into the vacuum as the best way to win her battle; the other had, without blinking, sacrificed everything so her daughter would have the best education. And Uyên herself had every intention of making both of these matter. "It's a dangerous game," Vân said.

A snort, from Uyên. "You say this when you're the one playing it best."

"I'm not," Vân said. Bitter laughter welled up in her: if she was playing it so well, why would the poetry club be throwing her out? "I can't really say I've been a success at it." The words welled out of her before she could stop them.

Uyên cocked her head at her. A silence: her eyes blinked, fast, as she accessed the network.

"I'm sorry," Vân said, horrified at her own impudence. "Please don't take what I said into account."

"Ah," Uyên said. Vân couldn't read the expression on her face. "The poetry club."

Vân's blood froze in her chest. "Child. How—"

Uyên laughed. "Second Mother has contacts at the tribunal and among the scholars." Her face changed again, hardened. Vân suddenly saw her first mother in her, ruthless and angry. She opened her mouth, but Uyên got there first.

"The poetry club are snobbish blinkered idiots."

Vân stared at her, aghast and not sure what she had heard. "Your mother—"

An eyeroll that was pure Uyên. "Teacher. Do you really think she's going to care about what a poetry club thinks of you?" A shrug. "That's assuming she finds out."

She couldn't possibly be suggesting… Vân's teacher instincts took over. "You owe respect to your elders."

Uyên bit her lip. Finally she said, "Respect doesn't mean slavish obedience. I *like* you, Teacher. I don't see why the poetry club would make any diffence." A pause, and just as Vân felt she couldn't be sinking any lower under the floor from sheer embarrassment, "Second Mother would want me to be taught by the best scholar in the Belt—and with your honoured ancestor in your brain, you could easily sit for the exam and get personally referred to the empress. You know you could."

Vân felt as though she'd fled from a dog only to run into a pack of tigers. She wanted to say that An Thành was not her own ancestor, that she'd made her from discarded bits of other people's ancestors, from the failed preservations she'd overseen as a student. The only thing that came out was a different kind of truth. "I wouldn't deserve it."

"Why?" Uyên's voice was sharp.

"Because she's too good," Vân said. "Because she'd be the one taking the exam, not me." Because she didn't have any *right* to Laureate An Thành—An Thành wasn't in her lineage, didn't extend any of her blessings from beyond the grave to her.

"So you think mem-implants are an unfair advantage?" Uyên asked. She had two, Vân knew: a Second and a Fourth Ancestor preserved from either side of her family.

Words crowded in Vân's thoughts. Yes, she wanted to say, as she'd said to Hương Lâm and Dinh when they'd been students in the poor, ramshackle state school, watching the wealthier candidates to the examinations stagger past them, their answers smooth and easy and never requiring more than a moment's thought—and she'd felt a burning envy, and a desperate need to have what they had. But, if she told Uyên the truth—if she admitted that her mem-implant wasn't her ancestor, that she had no qualifications, she'd lose Uyên's regard, if not her livelihood. What she'd done wasn't illegal, but it was unorthodox and scandalous—and Uyên's family, desperate for acceptance among the scholars, wouldn't tolerate it. "I think Laureate An Thành is a great comfort to me," she said. With An Thành, she finally had the surety and confidence she had craved—and she wasn't sure why, once spoken aloud, it felt curiously hollow. "But I don't want to take the examinations. I don't want to be at court. I'm not cut out for that kind of sky."

"And you think I am?"

Vân snorted. "You? Of course you are." Sharp and ruthless and ambitious, and utterly possessed of a sense of right and wrong. "Don't lie to me. That's what you've been breathing in since you were a child."

Uyên watched her, for a while. Then she said, carefully, as if lancing a wound gone bad, "First Mother should never have died."

"Ah." Vân exhaled.

"It was a necessary sacrifice, and it brought us the imperial grace. But we should never have had the Rơ so deep within our own territory." Her voice shook. No wonder.

"Scholars are allowed to criticise imperial policy. It's not sedition," Vân said, quietly.

"I don't want to criticise it," Uyên said. "I want to make it." Her face, flushed, was transfigured; she stood with her fists balled, looking Vân in the eye with no deference or respect. She was fierce and utterly compelling, the kind of leader people would follow into supernovas or fragmenting orbitals. Vân had never felt so proud of her.

"You will make it," Vân said. "I promise." It was foolish, something she couldn't even be sure to keep.

"Teacher." Uyên's face was taut. "Don't worry about the poetry club. Please. I'll sort it out if needed." She bowed down, more deeply than respect warranted, and something shifted and broke in Vân's chest.

Vân had been like that, once, burning with the desire to change things—not only her, but Hương Lâm and Dinh as well—drinking and talking way too much, trying to find their own way of defying the society that had failed them. Vân, working at the mem-implant maker and taking home the scraps of people's failed preservations to build Laureate An Thành under Hương Lâm's watchful eyes; and Dinh and Hương Lâm, always quick to laugh, always quick to rage— except they'd turned to crime to get back what they'd thought they were owed, and then it had all gone wrong and she hadn't stood by them, only watched as they were taken away, keeping her safe with their silence…

There was a sour taste in her mouth, like the one of the tea they'd drunk, back then; her hands tingling with the touch of mạt chược tiles after one too many games, after one too many poetry competitions based on the tiles' names—so many bad poems about the Nine of Infinities and the Eight of Threads, and the clacking of tiles like the chattering of sparrows…

A ping, from the network. The information Vân had requested on the house. Nothing of terrific interest, except…

"It's got interesting history," she said. "Did you know about who built the house?"

Uyên's face was blank, surprised. That was a no, then.

"Phạm Văn Ngọc Oanh, also known as Ngân Chi," Vân said. She read through the information. "Poet and architect. Known for her puzzles."

"Puzzles?" Uyên's voice was scornful. "Teacher, with all respect, is this the time for *games?*"

Vân bit back on the obvious, which was that Uyên herself enjoyed mạt chược and drinking games a little too much. "You missed the 'architect' part. She put her puzzles in the places she built."

Uyên stared at her. "Hiding places," she said, flatly. "Here?" She moved, staring at the walls. "Where—"

"I don't know. They say—" Vân's lips moved for a while, taking in the network's information—"they say she liked literary allusions." She looked at the examples laid out in front of her: how pressing on three carps in turn in a scene of a pond at night would cause the reflection of the moon to open, revealing a safe; how a willow branch in a portrait of a scholar could be pulled, revealing a secret room behind bookshelves. None of this seemed to apply to the small room they stood in.

"There are paintings…" Uyên looked dubious.

An Thành was quite happy to provide full context for the paintings: which scene of myth they represented, which scholar they portrayed. The room was a treasure-chest of portraits and allusions: way too many possibilities. She didn't even know what they were looking for—a safe, another room, an alcove to hide in? The examples she'd seen seemed obvious in retrospect, but hard to find without any clues. "Wait," she said. "The dead woman. Assuming she knew about the hiding place. Where was she?"

Uyên got up, and made a gesture. The River of Stars overlay shimmered back into existence for a brief moment—and then the corpse of the dead woman spread out over ever-shifting constellations. Then the overlay vanished, and the corpse—and just its imprint remained. It was pointing to a particular picture: a dragon spread over mountain slopes that descended all the way to the sea. A raging storm climbed from the shores to the mountain's slopes, and the dragon's antlers tangled with stars—a constellation that was briefly unfamiliar to Vân, before An Thành weighed in. *The Celestial River, in the Tail of the Azure Dragon.*

Which was not very helpful.

What did the river stand for? Forbidden love, in the story of the Cowherd and the Weaver. The tumults that separated the lovers, only bridged by magpies. And the dragon was a different kind of impossible love: the Dragon Lord of Lạc, who had married the immortal daughter of the mountain and found that she still yearned for her home, and he for the sea.

A hundred eggs, An Thành said, sharply.

I know the story. The daughter of the mountain had borne a hundred eggs out of which had hatched a hundred children. When they separated, she and the Dragon Lord had each taken half their sons back to their homes.

No, you don't understand. Look. In the dragon's mane.

In the intricate lacework of the dragon's mane, which fell from the mountains to the sea, were letters. Trăm. A hundred in Việt. Vân reached out, pressed them one by one. When she hit the last one, it sank into the painting with a click that resonated like an explosion—and an entire section of it swung inwards, a rectangle hidden amidst the storm on the shore.

A safe.

Vân let out a breath she wasn't aware she'd been holding. Uyên was watching her with awe in her eyes. "Teacher…"

"It's nothing," Vân said, obscurely embarrassed and obscurely proud.

She'd half-expected to find eggs in the safe, but of course dragons weren't likely to lay eggs in a small compartment in the Scattered Pearls Belt. Instead, what she pulled out were three things. The first was a piece of torn cloth that had been caught in the doorjamb when the safe had closed—the colour and hue of the dead woman's clothes.

"I didn't leave her alone that long," Uyên said with a frown. "But I guess it doesn't take that long, if you know how it works."

Vân snorted. "Harder to find, though." She spread the other two things on the table. One was a piece of something she didn't recognise—a smooth metal surface, like the substrate for a holo, except that it was blank. It was small: she could close her hand on it, and something about it was vaguely familiar, though she couldn't have said what. She and Uyên shook it, and couldn't make anything appear on it. "It's dead," Uyên said. "Or unprimed."

"Mmm," Vân said. She picked up the last thing in the safe. It was another piece of metal, shot through with oily reflections. "I don't think any of this was there in the first place. It's more likely she opened the safe and hid them inside, when she felt she was dying. Making sure the militia would never find them."

Uyên bit her lip. "I don't know what that last thing is, either."

Vân flipped it, watching the light play on it, again and again. "I do," she said. "Except that she couldn't have got it that easily."

"Illegal?" Uyên looked worried. The laws on receiving stolen goods were strict, and they assumed guilt rather than innocence.

"Not illegal, not per se. Just extremely hard to get without the right kind of help. It's from a dead mindship." She bit her lip. "Let me call *Sunless Woods*."

SUNLESS WOODS HAD been busy.

She hadn't exactly followed *Wine*'s advice, but she'd listened all the same. Some of her old crew was in the Scattered Pearls Belt, and quite receptive to be contacted.

One of them was Thiên Hoa.

Thiên Hoa was a bots-handler from the First Planet, the only one among them who could effortlessly claim something close to the accents of power. She had one mem-implant from a faraway ancestor who'd passed the regional examinations: her accent itself was subtly off, a mixture of her own and of the archaic one of the ancestor preserved in the mem-implant, but what the gang had needed was sometimes no more than a few moments of doubt to evade pursuers. Thiên Hoa had been enjoying life, not a scholar, but as a merchant in possession of rather more wealth than what she actually traded in.

She met *Sunless Woods* in one of the better teahouses in the belt: in the middle rings of the Apricot Blossom Hồ habitat, a delicate multi-story structure where each table was surrounded by just enough walls to ensure privacy.

Thiên Hoa slid into the booth, calling up a privacy overlay that shimmered around them: something that would block off the sound. "Well," she said. "That's fairly fancy, compared to our old haunts."

Sunless Woods had already ordered soup dumplings and rolled rice crepes. They'd appeared in her own overlay: she was chewing on the translucent dough dipped in fish sauce, getting faint and ghostly memories of her own childhood—the smell of squeezed lime on Mother's hands, the sharp taste of chilies as her siblings fought each other for the rolling pin—*Sunless Woods* had always preferred to help with the sauce, it was less drudgery and more of a chance of achieving that delicate balance between salty, acid and sweet...

Faint, very faint: nothing like the wave of nostalgia that had overwhelmed her when she'd tasted Vân's tea. It was for the best, all things considered. "How have you been?" she asked Thiên Hoa.

Thiên Hoa shrugged. Her bots rode in the jet-black mass of her hair, glinting in the light. "Oh, you know. Trying to get cargo from one end of the Empire to another. It's quite a challenge, actually." Her smile was wicked. "You?"

"I've been less bored," *Sunless Woods* said.

"Oh, I don't know," Thiên Hoa said. She grabbed one of the soup dumplings and brought it to her mouth. "Your little… problem certainly is unexpected."

Sunless Woods stiffened, and her own bots froze in answer. "How so?"

"The dead woman was hard to track. She knew all the tricks of evading surveillance. It's not illegal, per se…"

But it was certainly suggestive. "Go on."

"Best as I can see, she landed about two months ago on *The Goby in the Well*. And she didn't travel alone."

"She had a band." *Sunless Woods* exhaled. She wasn't sure if she was relieved or not.

"A small one," Thiên Hoa said. "Three other people. Three women."

"Mmm. And where are they now?"

A shrug from Thiên Hoa. "Hard to say. They seem to have vanished. I'll have some of my people look into tracking them."

Vanished, the better to regroup? To better plan whatever they'd had in mind. "I don't like this," *Sunless Woods* said.

A dazzling smile from Thiên Hoa. "Well, you're going to like that next bit."

"Out with it."

"Oh my, we're in a bad mood today, aren't we? Is it the scholar? *Wine* told me you had a soft spot for her."

Sunless Woods clamped down on an ill-tempered "none of your business", because she was the one who had made it Thiên

Hoa's business—and her friend was doing this as a favour to her. "Possibly," she said.

"Ah-ha. She's certainly pretty, and you could use a distraction."

Trouble was, *Sunless Woods* wasn't too sure the distraction was going to happen. Vân was worried about her own future and about Uyên, and sex was the last thing on her mind. "You were saying there was a bit I would like. I could use that." As opposed to hypothetical distractions whose chances of happening looked less and less.

"They've been around," Thiên Hoa said. "Your dead woman and her accomplices. Making inquiries in teahouses—the usual when trying to figure out the lay of the land and who's who in the militia, and how far they could go before being on their radar. But they were also drinking quite a fair bit—" a smile that was pure Thiên Hoa, all sharp teeth moments before she drove the knife in—"and let's just say they have no head for wine."

"Ah." *Sunless Woods* knew all about that, too. There was a reason the crew was on a strictly no-drinks policy when a job started. Wine was offered to other people, in the hope they'd misstep. "And you had ears."

"I can hardly be expected to do my job as a merchant if I don't keep abreast of what the criminal underclass is doing," Thiên Hoa said, with mock plaintiveness, and with the absolute confidence of one who firmly belonged in said criminal underclass. "Anyway…your dead woman boasted that they'd come here to steal a thing of great value."

"I'd gathered that," *Sunless Woods* said, drily. "Given that she defied an exile sentence to come back."

"Yeah." Thiên Hoa's eyes glittered. "Just think of it. We could grab it from right under their noses. Like the old days—a score big enough to make the news channels and the memorials, and all the scholars excoriating us for not upholding the order of Heaven and Earth…"

"I'm retired," *Sunless Woods* said, too quickly and too lightly.

"Yeah, right. And terminally bored, aren't you?"

It had been restful at first—not having to look over her shoulder for the militia, not having to worry about whether she or the rest of the gang would get caught and whether they'd get tortured to turn the others in. And then…before she knew it, she was a respectable pillar of society in more than name, a scholar invited to all the right banquets and all the right parties—all of it ringing tame and hollow, and she had that particular twitch that sent the bots scurrying back every time she went into someone's house and started cataloguing the things of value, and mentally mapping out where she'd have positioned her crew to clean everything out… And then, before she knew it, she'd become yesterday's news—none of the banquets so much as mentioned her, and other criminals were the frisson of high society.

No one had told her how much obscurity would *hurt*.

"I make do," *Sunless Woods* said, drily. But it'd be an honest job, wouldn't it? Finding long-disappeared treasure was headline material, and it didn't even require her to come out of retirement. She didn't even have to steal it: just to find it and return it to its rightful owners. The people would lap it all up—love her and her generosity with none of the ambiguity they'd had towards the thief.

Thiên Hoa's eyes shone in the darkness of their booth. "Don't lie."

"Fine," *Sunless Woods* said. "I'd notify the newscasters in a heartbeat if I found it. I guess it would belong to Uyên, which would be a nice flourish—the daughter of the graced war hero." Not that it mattered: she had enough wealth to satisfy her ten thousand times over, and she'd never stolen from those who badly needed funds. "Fame and adulation in one fell swoop."

"I don't think it belongs to Uyên, unless you're feeling generous." Thiên Hoa frowned. "Uyên's room was only the last of several places they visited. Whatever they were looking for, it's not specifically linked to Uyên. Here." She extended her hand, and an overlay shimmered into existence on the table, pushing away *Sunless Woods*'s teacup.

It was a haphazard list of places that didn't appear to have much in common with each other. The Great Western Compassion pagoda on the Apricot Blossom Hồ habitat, a Pavilion of the Meritorious on the Eastern Sea Trần habitat, a handful of private homes of which the Lotus Vũ's was the latest.

"I'm not sure…" *Sunless Woods* started, and then her comms showed her the call that had been waiting for her for a while. Vân. "Child?" she asked, sharing it with Thiên Hoa.

"I need help," Vân said. "To get onboard *The Elephant and Grass.*"

A pause. "I'm going to need a little more context," *Sunless Woods* said, equably.

The Elephant and Grass was a casualty of the Ten Thousand Flags uprising: a mindship who'd died, not in deep spaces, but simply in an inconvenient corner of space altogether, stuck in the midst of asteroids and debris that made access to her long-winded, requiring special equipment.

"There's a piece of that ship in Uyên's bedroom," Vân said, curtly. "In a secret safe."

Sunless Woods clamped down on the many obvious questions. "Are you sure? There are many mindship wrecks around the Belt."

"Yes," Vân said. "I have a mem-implant with a very good memory of recent Belt history. It's a piece of the hull, or somewhere exposed to starlight, and the pattern is characteristic." She sounded like she was indulging a child—and must have realised it. "Sorry, elder aunt."

"Don't be." In truth, *Sunless Woods* was fascinated—not only at the discovery, but at the way Vân, so usually staid and respectful, was forgetting herself. What else would it take, to make her blossom that way?

"It's a long story," Vân said. "Have you heard of Ngân Chi?"

Silver Branch? It sounded like a style name. *Sunless Woods* queried the network. "The architect? I fail to see…"

"She built the Lotus Vũ quarters," Vân said. "I mean, the quarters that the Lotus Vũ family now occupies. And she was the mother of *The Elephant and Grass*. I'd say that's one coincidence too many."

Thiên Hoa's face was a study in amusement. "Behave," *Sunless Woods* sent her, across the table. And then the name, Ngân Chi. *An architect.*

A pause. Thiên Hoa frowned. Her own eyes went slack as she accessed, first, her mem-implants, and then the network. She got her results faster than *Sunless Woods*, no doubt due to some highly personal and not entirely legal accesses to closed databases. Her answer came to *Sunless Woods* on a high-priority thread.

"It's not straightforward to find her name there, but she was involved in the Great Western Compassion Pagoda, and in all of these other buildings. Uh." A pause in Thiên Hoa's speech. "Was rumoured to have amassed a fortune in treasures—" images flashed across *Sunless Woods*'s field of vision, carved jade and delicate silver ornaments, and pearls and lacquered chests—"Except no one ever found anything. She died with only a few strings of coppers to her name."

"Well," *Sunless Woods* said, to Thiên Hoa, "I'd say dissipating money in old age is a fairly common occurrence, but the fact that our pair of thieves was searching all of Ngân Chi's buildings is suggestive." A theft to go down in history. That certainly would make ample news headlines, regardless of whether *Sunless Woods* kept the money or not.

"Mmm," Thiên Hoa said. "Are you going to tell her?"

"Not until we find out more," *Sunless Woods* said. For all she knew, it was a legend and nothing more, and she felt embarrassed promising to Vân something she wasn't sure she could deliver at all. And—if she was really honest with herself, and she usually was—she needed time to work out what she could do with this revelation, and how it changed things for her—or failed to. And, to Vân, "Why the ship? It's not the only place the dead woman visited."

"It's the only one she kept a piece of," Vân said. "That has to be significant."

"Mmm," *Sunless Woods* said. She stared at the list of buildings Thiên Hoa had found for her. The dead ship was easily the least accessible: a perfect hiding place? "All right. Let's go search the ship."

And, to Thiên Hoa, "I don't think finding the treasure will be the end of it. That woman died in Uyên's quarters, and her accomplices aren't going to let the matter rest."

Thiên Hoa's face was grave. "You want a word put out?"

Sunless Woods barely hesitated. "Yes. Don't use my name, but imply that Vân and Uyên, and their families, are under a greater protection, and that anyone who tries to kill them will have to answer to that."

Thiên Hoa's face was grave. "They will guess another thief is involved. I have to ask: are you sure? She's just a flirt. To reveal yourself, no matter how obliquely, to the militia…"

"No one's died on my watch," *Sunless Woods* said. "Either from us or the militia or anyone we took valuables from. We've not killed, and we've not let inaction kill anyone, either. I don't intend to start now."

VÂN SAT, STIFFLY, on the shuttle, her own bots clinging to her topknot, as rigid and as unmoving as she was.

"That's not quite what I had in mind," she said. She was trying very hard to prevent the excruciating flush growing in her from spreading to her face. Though *Sunless Woods* doubtless had bots and sensors and would likely sense her heightened body temperature.

Great. Just great.

Gentle laughter, echoing through the metal walls of the shuttle. "You asked for my help getting to a ship," *Sunless Woods* said. Her avatar coalesced in the room, leaning on the table that occupied most of it. "What did you think it was going to involve?"

She'd had no idea, to be honest. She'd thought that *Sunless Woods* was going to pull rank or favours or both to get them access to a spaceship—not that she was going to send one of her own shuttles to pick her up.

It was like any of the other shuttles that she'd taken: a square metal box with a table in the centre, and benches recessed into the sloping walls. The overlay was minimalist: just a few images of garlands of flowers.

Nevertheless, it was decidedly awkward, like being shown into someone's intimacy without the proper introductions.

"It's just a shuttle," *Sunless Woods* said. When she moved from the table to one of the benches, the stars outside the shuttle lingered under her feet. Vân found her breath hurting in her chest. "You're acting like I just disrobed in front of you." Laughter again. "Though that wouldn't have as much meaning for me as it would for you."

In spite of herself, Vân said, "You must have slept with humans."

"Some. We both have slightly different expectations about what this entails. It's all about making sure everyone's needs are amply…satisfied." The smile hadn't left *Sunless Woods*'s face. Vân felt her presence all around her, a palpable heartbeat running through the shuttle and through her own body. Then the ship grew serious. "We haven't had time to talk about the poetry club." A pause, then, "If you need another job, I'd be quite happy to recommend you for one."

"Oh." Vân felt herself turning beetroot red again. "Thank you. I don't think that will be necessary."

"Oh?"

"Uyên said the family wouldn't care about what happened with the poetry club."

A silence. Then the ship's hard, cutting voice. "Good. They shouldn't. And there are other clubs, if that's what you want."

"I don't know," Vân said. "Perhaps not right now." She saw again Uyên's hard face, heard her student's absolute certainty that she would sort things out.

My mother would want me to be taught by the best scholar in the Belt.

Except Uyên didn't know about An Thành, did she? She tried to breathe past the obstruction in her chest. "Shouldn't we be talking about the dead ship?"

"Mmm," *Sunless Woods* said. She shimmered in and out of existence, muttering to herself words that Vân could barely parse. *Star coordinates*, Laureate An Thành said.

Vân said, aloud, "Looking for something. You know, I don't much care about what it is they're after, as long as it's not Uyên. But there might be something on that ship that'll help us track her companions down."

A pause. *Sunless Woods* said, at last, "You know, they didn't find what they were looking for in Uyên's room. They might let the matter rest."

"Might? Be honest, elder aunt. We have a corpse in Uyên's room—not only that, but one so deeply modified the militia hasn't been able to identify it. Which means no proper funeral rites, and no burial with the rest of her family." Vân shook her head. "They might have come here to steal, but now it's going to be about revenge." And it was going to be ugly.

They needed to track down the accomplices and turn them over to the militia before that happened.

When she looked up again, the ship's avatar was sitting next to her, and *Sunless Woods*'s bots were on both her shoulders, gently squeezing—it was like being held in a ghostly embrace. "You're upset."

"Uyên being a target of some shadowy underworld's revenge wasn't on my priority list, no," Vân said, stiffly. Warmth was spreading to her shoulders and spine, an odd breathless kind of feeling she couldn't quite name.

"I was going to say you don't have to do this, but you would do it anyway, wouldn't you?"

"She's my student," Vân said, simply. "I have obligations to her."

"Most teachers would wash their hands of this."

"I'm not most teachers." It sounded stiff and boastful, and she clamped her lips on what she might have said afterwards. *It's true, though*, An Thành said.

The silence that spread afterwards was awkward, but Vân was used to awkwardness. She'd gotten plenty of it as one of the only poor students in the state school. *Sunless Woods* was

back to navigating, speaking to herself again, and the garlands of flowers fluttered in an invisible wind.

"We're here," *Sunless Woods* said.

EVEN THE SHUTTLE couldn't make it that far into the debris field that surrounded *The Elephant and Grass*. Vân suited up instead, grabbing one of the shadow-skins behind the benches to protect her against the vacuum—if being in one of *Sunless Woods*'s shuttles was like the ship disrobing to her, she amply repaid *Sunless Woods* when she put the shadow-skin on: taking off all the clothes in a half-alcove that was all the privacy the ship could afford her, her bots helping her latch the comms module and making sure her topknot didn't get caught in the skin's folds.

"I'm not looking," *Sunless Woods* said. She sounded amused again. "You're not the first to change clothes here, you know."

"How many of these did you sleep with?"

The same gentle laughter. "A question I won't answer, I fear. But I have done some work as a civilian transport, in another life. I've had my share of passengers."

But she wasn't doing it anymore. Which begged the question of what she lived on, exactly. Maintaining a ship was expensive, which was why most mindships were in the service of the empire, or in freight transports where the ability to jump into deep spaces and cut short long slow journeys served them well. What did *Sunless Woods* do for a living? She was a scholar, to be sure; but Vân knew all too well that being a scholar didn't pay the bills.

Family wealth, An Thành said, gently.

That had to be it.

Nevertheless…nevertheless, her demeanour was off. Vân had hung around enough children of the powerful in her youth, and *Sunless Woods* didn't act like any of them. Perhaps a family that had only recently become wealthy?

And why was it any of her business anyway? The ship had been nothing but helpful; and obviously Vân had to wonder about motive—but the why of it was transparent enough, wasn't it—and would she quibble, really, if things got that far?

This time, the flush started in her belly, and spread to her cheeks and the tips of her fingers. She crossed her legs, but it just made matters worse.

"Child? Child?"

"Sorry," Vân said, colouring again. "Daydreaming."

"I can see that." Again, that repressed laughter. "On to more serious things: I won't be able to project an avatar once you leave the ship. But I can guide you."

"Radio comms?"

"My bots, if you'll have them."

"Why would I not?"

A silence. "I can see how that'd be awkward." Bots were highly personal, after all. Vân snorted.

"We've come this far. I'd be lacking common sense if I turned away now."

A charged silence. "It's not dangerous," *Sunless Woods* said. "You're small and more mobile than a ship. It'll just take time. You need to be patient."

"That's why no one has gone to retrieve *The Elephant and Grass?*" She was thinking of funerals and of burials—where did they put the dead ships, were there mausoleums large enough to contain the whole of their bodies?

They compact them, Laureate An Thành interjected. *And burn them if they cannot. Some have been left as living mausoleums in space, but it's inconvenient for their descendants to visit.*

"Mmm," *Sunless Woods* said. "That, and how she died. Multiple explosions left her hull badly damaged. Even if we got her out of the debris she'd likely come apart from the stress of being hauled. And she was pretty thoroughly destroyed, and transporting nothing of value and no passengers—so not worth the time or expenses."

"She must be so terribly lonely," Vân said, before she could think. "Drifting in the dark with no one to tend to her grave. Did she—did she have family, at least?" Some holo somewhere on some ancestral altar, some respects and prayers sent her way.

"I don't know." *Sunless Woods* sounded startled. "She had siblings, so I assume she has descendants. But Ngân Chi's family was penniless, so they wouldn't have had money to spare for a salvage operation." A pause.

"You think I'm weird," Vân said, defensively.

"Not at all." *Sunless Woods*'s voice was pensive, her avatar barely there at all, just an outline almost merging with the metal walls. "I think most people wouldn't have cared about what happened to a long-dead ship." The shuttle shuddered, as if it were coming apart—and one of the benches seemed to collapse on itself—scrunching itself tightly until it revealed the darkness of space. "There. That's your airlock. Let's go pay our respects."

IT WAS ODD, being out there.

Like almost everyone in the Belt, Vân had received basic security training which included space mobility as well as handling the various protective suits from the old metal shells to the newer shadow-skins; and, like almost everyone in the Belt, she'd never had to use that training.

It came back to her as she launched—the particular way every movement would carry her much further than she'd expected, how she'd turn and spin, keeping at bay her brain's atavistic panic that she was falling, trying to remember where she put her up and her down, and to find a reference point in the asteroids around her. The shadow-skin clung to her clothes like a damp shirt, and the only sound was that of her breath. In her hands was the glider she'd use to weave her way around asteroids, securely clamped to one of her wrists: a metal heaviness that felt both familiar and utterly alien, like a half-remembered thing from a dream. And in her ears a faint sound: a half-remembered, rhythmic thing that felt like the edge of a poem in a dream, an overlapping chorus of radio waves coming from the sun and the stars and everything around her.

"You're doing very well," *Sunless Woods* said.

She turned, briefly—saw the shuttle outlined in the glare of the sun, metal glinting on its facets; felt the faint scritching of bots on the shadow-skin, like a ghostly touch. She was warm again, her heartbeat easing down. Within her, Laureate An Thành was silent—not interjecting anything, but simply drinking in the view.

She turned on the glider. Its rumble spread to her wrists and arms: she lay down and nudged herself into position, gently nosing between the asteroids—they seemed so small seen from far away, children's rocks, and then as she got closer they dwarfed her, growing from small fist-sized specks to huge craggy walls around her.

"Slowly. Any hit you take is going to be linked to their speed and yours."

Two centidays in, she saw the ship. It was nothing special, at first: a speck that seemed like all the other specks scattered around her—and then as she got closer, weaving her way through the various scattered debris, it grew and grew, from a speck into a sleek silhouette—and then, as the glider carried her closer, what had looked like the outline of a ship became a confused, broken jigsaw of pieces hanging together in some mysterious alchemy—the forces that had blown them apart in the first place now spent, and their own gravity, and the distant ones of the more massive asteroids, drawing them into unfathomable patterns—An Thành was in her thoughts, trying to bring forth poetry on the vagaries of space and struggling; but it didn't matter because that distant symphony of the stars was there, filling her to bursting.

She passed one more asteroid, nudging the glider past the floating debris—no longer rocks but leftovers of the explosion that had torn the ship apart: bits of oily metal, fragments of motors and painted walls. It felt like going through a graveyard: a particular kind of mausoleum with only one occupant, broken and stretched thin.

Unbidden, the name of the Buddha of Infinite Splendor came to her lips, as if she were attempting to meditate, except on the ship's behalf.

Nam mô A Di Đà Phật, Nam mô A Di Đà...

Over and over until her mind went into a trance—and the ship growing larger and larger around her—now she was deep inside its ruins, and the profound silence was that of the grave—and all she could see was a splayed corpse.

"I have no idea where our dead woman went," she said, aloud.

One of the bots crawled closer to her face, gripped the top of her ear. "I do," *Sunless Woods*'s voice said. An overlay shimmered on top of Vân's field of vision, showing a faint trail. "That's the trail of her glider."

"Heat? Surely…"

"Not heat. The remnants of the elements it burnt to get there. It's an unusual enough activity in the vicinity that I'm able to pick them up. Hang on…" *Sunless Woods* did something, and the trail coalesced into something harder and more luminous—though it widened faintly as it went on. "I'm a little more uncertain once she slowed down: the pattern is more spread out and fainter. Hopefully I'll be able to refine it somewhat if you get closer."

The curve arced through one of the largest pieces of debris in the field. Vân nudged her own glider forward, towards the gaping hole in its centre.

"You said there was a hidden safe," *Sunless Woods* said.

"Yes," Vân said. Up close, the hull looked as if a giant, distorted flower of metal had burst outwards from the heart of the ship—and behind that hole was a vast, profound darkness in which nothing lived or breathed, a silence more final than that of stars or planets. Vân toggled, with a flick of her fingers, the light on her own glider. It illuminated a large structure that looked like a hangar, with the scattered debris of shuttles, and a single bloodied thread linking each of them back to the ship.

The trail of light went through the hangar, and through a small space at the other end—a door, Vân realised, something that suddenly made sense and was at her scale. "You think she hid another safe in the ship?"

Sunless Woods said, "I don't know. It's one thing to modify a habitat. A ship is a living body, as you can see. It'd be a little like someone opening up your chest to safeguard valuables: unpleasant, and risky."

"But—"

"But?"

"Surely the rooms in the ship were built." And then she stopped. It would have been before, wouldn't it—when the Mind in the ship's heartroom was still incubated in her mother's belly, and a Master of Wind and Water went over this ship, making sure everything was perfect, that the khi-elements flowed the proper way in every corridor and hangar and storeroom. Before the birth and the implantation of the Mind in the body that had always been meant for her—before she came alive and grew up yearning for the stars under whose light she died. "The mother doesn't design the ship's body, does she?"

A pause. "It's unusual. But not impossible." *Sunless Woods* was grudgingly impressed.

"I don't understand what they hope to find in those safes." Vân had checked: the architect had died five years ago—around the time Vân was designing Laureate An Thành. An uneasy coincidence—she'd had to breathe hard after finding that out, but of course so many things had happened that year across the Belt. And there'd been nothing of note in that death.

Sunless Woods said, casually, "I imagine something of value. It's always tempting."

"To rob the dead? Or her descendants? That's just…" Cowardly. Illegal, yes—but also profoundly disrespectful.

Another bot had climbed on her shoulder, as if the ship were standing right there, gripping it again—trying to comfort her, a touch that made her flushed and yearning. At length, "I'm sorry," *Sunless Woods* said. "I shouldn't have brought it up. It was in poor taste." Vân was used to pity, or condescension, open questioning of her common sense—but this sounded almost like…envy?

"It's all right," she said. "I have impossibly high standards."

A lengthier silence. She'd reached the door now: she pushed the glider up, so that she could stand in the corridor behind it. For a bare moment she was, not in a ruin, not in a corpse or a mausoleum, but in a darkened ship, the walls glistening with paintings of starscapes and waterfalls, with calligraphied texts. For a bare moment she felt wind whistle in her ears, and saw the walls slowly contract under the beat of a giant heart. And then it passed, and she was once more in the shipwreck, the paintings nothing more than faint splashes, the walls utterly still, the space around her nothing but vacuum with not a trace of wind.

Her comms blinked. It looked like a call from Uyên. "Child?" she asked. Uyên's voice came back excited and garbled—fragments of words scythed into nothingness by the distance. "I don't have network where I am." And she cut it off, hoping Uyên would at least get that.

The trail arced through the corridor, and finally ended at a door that wouldn't budge no matter how hard Vân or the bots tried to tug at it.

"It's warped in the explosion." *Sunless Woods* sounded faintly irritated. "Hang on. The bots don't have enough strength, but I can find something else…"

But the dead woman had still managed to get through it. Which meant there was a way. Or that she'd had some industrial equipment with her? Had she come prepared, for whatever she'd hoped to take from the ship? If her accomplices had been with her, it should have been easier to wield heavier objects.

This close, the trail of light was a muddled soup of faint radiance. "Can you show me where she was?"

An irritated snort from *Sunless Woods*. "I don't have enough evidence."

A probability map, Laureate An Thành said, gently. Vân repeated that aloud, and felt shock ripple through the ship—catching even the bots, which stilled for a brief moment, even the ones on her shoulder and ear.

"You're not an engineer," *Sunless Woods* said.

"I am. And so is my mem-implant," Vân said, before she could stop herself. She wouldn't lie and say that An Thành had been an engineer, because An Thành hadn't existed before Vân had cobbled her together. But the wording was suggestive, and *Sunless Woods* was observant. Vân was flirting with disaster.

She waited, her heart in her chest. But *Sunless Woods* merely said, "Hmmm" in that peculiar way of hers, and something gradually shimmered into existence in her overlay: a field of light that was strongest where the probabilities of presence were highest. It shone brightest in two areas: one right to the door, which yielded nothing in particular. The other was a few forelengths from the door. Vân pushed her glider forward, cursing as she overcompensated for the motion and almost smashed into the other wall. When she finally righted herself and pushed the glider upright once more, she was staring at alcoves that looked like the pigeonholes of a library. They were oddly disposed in an elongated diamond: the largest number of them in the centre, and then a tapering off to two points towards ceiling and bottom of the corridor. The death of the ship had shrivelled the pigeonholes inwards, and they glittered with frost. Once, they'd been labelled, but the letters were so faint Vân could barely make them out. They had no books on them, which suggested that the books had either been overlay, or that they'd been taken—no, wait. A single one of the holes contained a stiff, frozen roll—not paper but metal, which displayed a title in sharp lights when Vân's suited hand brushed it.

Destiny woven with Talent.

Quite likely Tale of Kiều, An Thành said. *A pre-Exodus work.* And, when Vân didn't react she quoted the opening lines:

Within the hundred years that we all live through
Destiny and talent are woven in bitter struggle

Mulberry fields stretching into vast seas…

Dâu. Mulberry—that metaphor was for upheavals of life, the land turning into the sea—but dâu also meant a daughter-in-law. Vân looked, again, at the peculiar arrangement of the shelves. Her hand brushed the faded letters, which she now knew the nature of. *Father. Mother.* "It's a family tree," she said. "A diagram of degrees of mourning. That's why it's so wide at the centre, where the web of relationships is thickest: siblings, cousins, parents' siblings, ascendants and descendants…" She found the one corresponding to the bride of a son, rummaged in it. Something shifted and clicked.

The door irised open, expanding outwards until it had disappeared into the wall. Vân slid the glider down, preparing to lie down again so she could be propelled through the door. "Wait," *Sunless Woods* said, sharply. The bots fell away from her, scuttled towards the opening. "You have no idea what's beyond that door." And then a spreading silence. "All clear, but—"

"But what?" Vân was already pointing her glider towards the door; going through as easily as a welding-blade through metal. Beyond the door was some kind of passenger room, with a recessed bed, and a table—everything must have been in overlay, so what remained was oddly desolate, the veins in the walls the colour of celadon—and in the wall, above the bed, a large rectangular shape that had to be Ngân Chi's secret safe, where most of *Sunless Woods*'s bots were congregating—surely it would be empty, but perhaps the dead woman had left a trail they could find, like they'd followed the piece of hull to the dead ship…

"Child." *Sunless Woods*'s voice was sharp, almost wounding. "Get out. Now."

The bots fled the safe, a flood of scalded ants, pushing the door open in their panic to scatter—and in that revealed opening Vân finally saw what had been stuffed inside, and why it was still there.

It was a corpse.

They had been wearing a shadow-skin: their death had disintegrated it, and it hung around them in loose filaments. Their body hung at impossible angles. Bones must have been broken to put them there. Vân saw all this with almost clinical detachment—because it would have been pointless to panic, because she couldn't seem to catch her breath, because she could feel *Sunless Woods*'s own panic in the way that her bots incoherently scattered, in the fast, heavy heartbeat in her own ear, coming from the body of the ship—because there was a layer of iced blood around the corpse, like a stiffened macabre suit.

"Teacher? Teacher, are you there?" Uyên's voice in her ears, except that Vân couldn't seem to drag up words to answer her.

I'm busy. I can't talk to you right now.

Wait, please.

"You know that thing we found in the safe? The thin silver of metal you couldn't figure out? It's a mạt chược tile, with the artist's signature—not the regular game chips but an ornamental one to carry in a sleeve, or put on a bedside table. It was encoded, that's why it didn't display anything."

Wait.

Vân's own bots were unfolding the corpse: no features beyond a layer of ice so thick she couldn't make out anything. It looked unreal, like a doll, the movements of its limbs stiff and difficult—blood icicles breaking out and floating around it.

"The contamination danger..." *Sunless Woods* said, but Uyên was speaking again, and her words were as sharp as blades.

"Teacher, can you hear me? It's the Seven of Threads, and it was painted by someone called Hương Dinh. I've called in a favour from one of Second Mother's friends at the tribunal, and they've confirmed what remains of the dead woman's genetic material matches Lê Thị Hương Dinh's."

Hương Dinh.

Dinh.

Hương Lâm.

Seven of Threads, Seven of Infinities, Seven of Barrels.

Vân was twenty-one again, sitting in their garret in the Sword Turtle habitat, with their own clothes pasted at the window to keep out the cold until maintenance could fix the insulation—which they all knew wasn't going to happen any time soon, so they were drinking rice wine to keep warm. Vân was holding the mạt chược tiles, looking into Hương Lâm's thin, sharp face—and hearing Dinh's voice, as she stared at the pile of discards, where three Seven tiles shone in the light, the crude painting flaking off the patterns. "They're just like us, aren't they? Poor mismatched sods that no one really values."

She'd forgotten it, in the wake of the arrest. The tiles, the way they'd styled themselves with their names for a while, pleased with their own pathetic cleverness.

"They're dead," she said, aloud. They'd been sent to the closest numbered planet to await their sentencing at the Autumn Assizes, and there had been no imperial amnesty that year. "They're dead!"

"Child?" *Sunless Woods*'s voice was distant, and receding with every passing moment. "Child!"

Three of Vân's bots spun out of control: the arm they were trying to unfold snapped in half, revealing glistening muscle and veins, like meat in a compartment freezer—a sound like the roar of a waterfall in Vân's ears, growing and growing until it seemed to take over the entire world—until nothing was left but the corpse's pale, distorted, unrecognizable shape—and Hương Lâm's face as the militia led her away.

They're dead. They've always been, always been…

Everything spun and spun, and blurred away into nauseous and unfathomable darkness.

SUNLESS WOODS WATCHED as her bots crawled over the body. She wasn't squeamish—she'd lived through the uprising, and seen her share of dead bodies. Never killing didn't protect her against death.

She'd had the bots take it back to one of the sterile chambers in her own body, and thoroughly decontaminated everything that had touched it, from shuttle to bots. Now she was overseeing an autopsy: the bots could have done it themselves, without her direct supervision, a low-level task on a low-priority thread that required no attention from her.

It did, however, serve to keep her occupied.

The bots cut away the remnants of the shadow-skin: in death it had fragmented into blood-stained filaments, saving her the trouble of having to deal with the bloated layer of blood and other body fluids that would have filled the shadow-skin—but also dispersing said fluids all over the ship's room. *Sunless Woods* had been too busy wrangling the emergency of Vân's life at stake to collect *these*.

The corpse was a woman of uncertain age—early nineties or a hundred, *Sunless Woods* would have said, perhaps more: she could track the rejuv treatments in the folds of the wrists and the faint lines on the teeth, marking when the enamel had been regenerated. Old, but not ancient yet.

She'd died of multiple stab wounds: one of them had nicked the descending aorta, and there were kidney lacerations as well. All on the back: there was no sign of struggle anywhere. She had trusted whoever had done this enough to turn her back on them—mind you, she had trusted them enough to trek with them to a dead mindship in the middle of nowhere.

On her comms, only silence; broken by the faint scuttling of the bots, and the sharp feel of the corpse's skin on their claws. *Sunless Woods* thought, for a while, watching the woman's still face—bruised and made almost unrecognisable by death and its long sojourn in space. The murder weapon wasn't clear: whatever it was, it had sheared through the shadow-skin like it didn't exist. Some kind of tool; except something that had been modified to actually cut through the shadow-skin. Which meant it was black-market and sold to criminals.

She opened a comms line to Thiên Hoa. "Lil'sis?"

"Mmm." Thiên Hoa shimmered in overlay in *Sunless Wood*'s perception, translucent and distant. She was kneeling in her library, looking for a scroll. "Account books. You wouldn't believe the amount of record-keeping one has to do as an honest merchant. Frankly, there are advantages to a life of crime."

In spite of herself, *Sunless Woods* was amused. "Less paperwork? Really?"

"That's because you've never had to file taxes in three different jurisdictions," Thiên Hoa said, darkly. "And don't get me started on the employees' paperwork. Anyway…what can I do for you, big'sis?"

"Can you take a look at this?" *Sunless Woods* said, and granted Thiên Hoa visual access to the dead woman's corpse.

"Uh." Thiên Hoa was silent. "Can you do three-dee?" After *Sunless Woods* had upgraded her access, Thiên Hoa materialised in the room. She knelt, watching the dead woman's face carefully. At length, she rose, brushing her hands on her embroidered tunic. "Are you thinking what I'm thinking?"

"I don't know," *Sunless Woods* said. She called up the picture of Architect Ngân Chi again, stared at it. "How long ago did you say she died again?"

"Nah," Thiên Hoa said, lapsing away from her refined speech patterns. "Ngân Chi died in her bed five years ago, of a prolonged illness that left her bed bound. I mean, even assuming the militia had been mistaken on the identity of the corpse they declared dead, there's no way Ngân Chi would have put on a shadow-skin and gone traipsing on a dead spaceship. But…" She pursed her face, the way she always did when facing a particularly thorny problem. Thiên Hoa's approach to problems was to latch on to them and keeping worrying at them until they shrivelled away to nothing. "Hmmmm. Her second younger cousin Ái Hồng on the father's side is in the right age band." Her mouth moved, for a while, though no sounds came out. "Let's see…yeah, what I thought. No one has reported anything, but she hasn't been pinging the network for a few days."

Which wasn't a good outlook. "Are you sure?"

"Who can be sure of anything?" Thiên Hoa shrugged. "The descriptions match, down to the rejuv treatments."

"So what do we think? That Ái Hồng came down here looking for her cousin's money and it turned badly?"

Thiên Hoa made a noise through her noise. "Well, she *was* poor. Her parents were never very wealthy, and they lost the little they had in the Ten Thousand Flags uprising. And she was a power-hungry little bastard, wasn't she—growing up without any food or money will do that to you." It was said almost affectionately, with that self-deprecating tone that made it clear Thiên Hoa was partly referring to her own childhood.

Sunless Woods said, "You never stole from a relative." She wasn't sure if that was comforting to Thiên Hoa or not.

"Because I'm not lacking common sense," Thiên Hoa said, sharply. "Stealing from a relative is stiffer penalties." She cocked her head at *Sunless Woods.* "Are you expecting me to be filial?"

She was, for all her bluster—sending, quietly, money to her aged mother on the First Planet, which was then passed on to the rest of her elderly aunts and uncles. But she'd also quite cheerfully claw *Sunless Woods*'s eyes out if *Sunless Woods* pressed her point. "Back to our dead woman."

"The first, or the second? Sorry." Thiên Hoa lowered her eyes for a brief moment. "That was too far. I take it you mean Ái Hồng. I can enquire, but we can safely say she hadn't found Ngân Chi's cache, else she would have been more profligate with money over the last five years."

"So she was looking for it. And the other woman was too?"

"She came to Uyên's house after the first murder. I'd say she intended to incapacitate Uyên and then search the room, but she saw an opportunity when Uyên left."

"Mmm. And she committed the first murder? That of Ái Hồng?"

Thiên Hoa's face was grave. "Almost certainly," she said. "Look at the wounds."

"I've seen them," *Sunless Woods* said.

"That's a vacuum blade. The instrument maintainers use for minute cuts to metal when repairing a habitat." She pointed to the shadow-skin: *Sunless Woods*'s bots scuttled over, their sensors zooming in on the burn marks around the cut. "You'll have matching burn marks on her, too—less easily seen because of all the bruising and freezing. You'll remember the dead woman in Uyên's room had burn marks on her hands."

A silence. *Sunless Woods* broke it. "Amateur," she spat. She wasn't sure what made her angrier: the lack of thought, or the death of Ái Hồng, or both. "She used a blade that cuts through shadow-skin and never thought it'd burn through her own protection."

"Yeah, that's what you get when people turn to crime without the proper training." Thiên Hoa's face was grave, but her voice was taut, angry. "No forethought and no drive."

"I don't know." *Sunless Woods* manifested near the dead woman in her usual avatar, feet resting lightly on the floor by Thiên Hoa's side. She looked down at the corpse, trying to think of something, of anything that would bring it all into sharp focus. "She seemed pretty driven to me. She came back in spite of the exile-implants. That much money is worth fraud, or even murder, isn't it?"

"You say this like you're considering it. At least the non-murdering part."

Sunless Woods grimaced. It was an odd feeling: she saw the change of colours across her own walls while also feeling it deep in her own body—not that often that she had people on board. "You know I'm not. Framing someone for a grave crime is as good as murder. They have an overwhelming chance of being executed or exiled, and the militia wouldn't take precautions. They'd just pressure and torture them into a confession, regardless of whether any of it is true."

"Look at you." Thiên Hoa's voice was fond. "Firebrand."

"Always. My position hasn't changed."

"Mm. Anyway, I don't have our little band of thieves yet, but this changes things." Thiên Hoa smiled, wickedly, the way she did when vicariously enjoying *Sunless Woods* verbally tearing people to shreds—"A murder investigation is a serious thing, and a lot of people won't want that heat. They'll talk. And then we'll have them."

Sunless Woods thought of the body—of the vacuum blade biting into the shadow-skin, of blood spurting, spreading, of every organ shutting itself while the suit desperately scrambled to maintain integrity; and of the indignity of it stuffed in a safe with no one to mourn or propitiate their ancestor's spirit as it fled towards Hell. "Good," she said. "And I'll take great pleasure in delivering them to the militia in a neat little package."

"Though not before relieving them of their valuables."

"The treasure?"

"Yes. The one you're very carefully not telling Vân about."

"Careful," *Sunless Woods* said. Her voice was cold: a warning to Thiên Hoa she was pushing it too far, that she remained the eldest in their band and its leader. That she wouldn't be questioned on her questionable decisions. "I'm not telling her about the treasure because as of now, it doesn't exist. It's killed two people, and neither appears to have much enjoyed riches prior to their deaths. Do you really think it's worth worrying her to death for a mirage?" But she *wanted* to tell Vân. She wanted to present her and Uyên with riches beyond their wildest dreams; to see the shock on Vân's face as she realised she no longer needed to hide anymore, that she didn't need to scrimp and bow down to society to earn a living.

She'd make that happen, and then she'd disappear again, if need be, if it got too hot for her. She'd take on another identity and another face in another system, and find another way to pass the time.

"Aw. Look at you. All caring and concerned." Thiên Hoa's face softened. "It's been such a long time since you allowed yourself to be like that."

"Shut up," *Sunless Woods* said. And knew she'd said too much, or not enough, when her friend rose and cocked her head at her, thoughtfully—as if *Sunless Woods* were the problem and not the corpse.

"You brought her here, didn't you? On your ship."

"My body," *Sunless Woods* said, mildly.

"You know what I mean. When's the last time you've brought one of your flirts here?"

"There was no choice," *Sunless Woods* said. Vân had passed out, mumbling incoherent syllables in her sleep. Her shadow-skin—*Sunless Woods*'s shadow-skin, because it had come from one of her shuttles—was covered in blood and gore and various body fluids. She'd needed a check-up, and *Sunless Woods* wasn't going to leave it to some cheap doctor on-station—because that was what Vân would insist on for fear of not being able to afford it, and while *Sunless Woods* could go full auntie on her, it was much easier to spare herself the argument in the first place.

Sunless Woods had been very carefully holding herself in check—not looking at the room where she'd left Vân sleping, under the grip of a mild sedative, and with bots on an automated watch of her vitals. She could let it all happen on a thread she was barely aware of, not calling the visuals or audio or anything that would make her fully, consciously present.

"First corpse?" Thiên Hoa asked, and then shook her head. "It's her second, isn't it?"

"Mmm," *Sunless Woods* said. "The first one wasn't as gruesome, I should think."

"Ah." Thiên Hoa nodded, sagely. "It's not every day you find a body stuffed in a chest."

They had, and other things besides—limbs and torn-off fingernails and eyeballs—and once, memorably, enough vials of blood to empty a body twice over. *Sunless Woods* had called the heist off and they'd quietly tipped off the militia—who'd followed the blood's owner to a quiet patch of earth on the Twenty-Fifth Planet, which turned out to be the burial grounds of a rather busy murderer. The Measure of Bones Killer, they'd dubbed him when they'd finally caught him, using the word that meant field and earth and village at the same time.

"Mmm," *Sunless Woods* said. "She kept repeating 'they're dead'. I suppose it makes sense." Certainly the gender had matched. But…

Thiên Hoa watched her for a while. "Spit it out," she said. "Something is bothering you."

Sunless Woods hesitated. "It's the tone. Like she'd personally known them."

"But she didn't, right?"

"No," *Sunless Woods* said. "The first body didn't mean anything to her."

"Mmm." Thiên Hoa didn't say anything. She didn't need to. The first body had been so thoroughly altered even her own

mother wouldn't have recognised her. "Well, there is an easy solution to your problem."

"Really?"

"Yes." Thiên Hoa's voice was deadpan. "It's called go and talk to her."

Sunless Woods felt as though someone was squeezing her bloodless—which was ridiculous, because the core of her was impregnable, a Mind hugging connectors in a locked and sealed heartroom deep in the bowels of the ship—like a brain in a human skull, something no one would ever touch unless there was cause. "No," she said.

A snort from Thiên Hoa. "Really? You're backing away from a challenge? You? The thief who sneaked into the Purple Forbidden City to grab the Fifth Emperor's celadon set? The one who infiltrated the Imperial Censorate and falsified official seals so she could free her crew from penal servitude?"

"I'm not afraid." But she was, and she wasn't even sure why. It wasn't Vân. She could run rings around her—Vân wasn't a good liar, wasn't fast on her feet, wasn't the kind of person who effortlessly adapted to anything and everything. And yet…and yet, she'd marched into the bare house determined to save her student, and had dragged *Sunless Woods* onto the corpse of *The Elephant and Grass*. And yet…and yet, she was fundamentally, profoundly honest, ringing as sharp and as whole as a pagoda bell—and *Sunless Woods* found she didn't know what to do with any of that anymore.

Thiên Hoa didn't say anything. She didn't need to. She just watched *Sunless Woods* with that sharp, ironic smile on her face, the same one she'd always had prior to a heist, when everything was so taut it felt a storm was going break; Hải's children were at each other's throats, and *Wine* was busying herself by making wounding remarks aimed at anyone who so much as moved.

"Fine, fine," *Sunless Woods* said. "I'll go and talk to her."

IN VÂN'S JUMBLED, broken dreams, she was younger, bent over the table where she was piecing her mem-implant together—watched over by ghosts and ancestors, all with the same faint expression of disapproval, and billowing in a non-existent wind like the banners of an invisible army . She was sitting alone in the militia interrogation room, her arm aching where the injector had gone into it—and Laureate An Thành emerged from the shadows to look at her, except that she wasn't wearing the robes and jade belt of a scholar, but the white áo dài of a young girl, and her hair was unbound, trailing down her shoulders and pooling on the floor like an oil slick, merging with the shadows of the room. *I know*, Vân wanted to say, but the words tasted like shrivelling ice in her mouth, and when An Thành looked up her emaciated, bruised face was that of the corpse in the secret safe, was that of Hương Lâm when they'd taken her away.

We protected you, big'sis. Don't go and waste it all.

She woke up with a start, in a darkened, unfamiliar room. Her heartbeat felt like it would burst through her chest. The shadow-skin she'd been wearing was gone, and she wasn't wearing nearly enough clothes—just a flimsy, translucent shirt and trousers embroidered with lotus flowers that didn't stop the faint wind in the room from raising goosebumps on her skin. Recycled air, and it was too sharp and too slightly stale to be a habitat, unless it was one of the smaller outermost ones. Her bots lay on the floor in a tangled mess: they were gradually waking up, becoming available for her commands. Which meant she'd been unconscious for long enough they'd deactivated.

She—

Where was she?

"Good morning," *Sunless Woods* said. The ship was leaning against one of the walls—Vân could have sworn she hadn't been there before. "Feeling better?"

She felt nauseous, and hungry, and wholly out of sorts, but the only thing that came out of her mouth was, "I'm fine."

"You are demonstrably not." The ship had changed: her avatar wasn't quite within human proportions anymore—limbs too long, body stretched towards the ceiling—the stars that had trailed the wake of her gestures now visible even when she was at rest—and in her eyes, an oily sheen that was that on the walls and on the floor.

Certainty hit her like a punch in the gut. "You brought me to you. To your body." It wasn't habitat air she was breathing—she was on a mindship. On *Sunless Woods*. Now that her own heartbeat had slowed down she could hear the faint sound—the steady beat that drew faint, translucent patterns on the walls, that oily sheen that seemed to tremble on everything, and to spread every time she turned away from it…

This was way worse than the shuttle.

"Yes." *Sunless Woods* face was grave. "I apologise. It was the simplest." She moved, fluid, fast, stood at Vân's side—a mere forelength away, close enough that the odd heat of her presence trembled in the air between them. "You were covered in blood and less savoury body fluids. The corpse was frozen, but Heaven knows what kind of bacteria developed in the time it's been on *The Elephant and Grass*."

The corpse. Vân tried, very hard, to dispel the memory of that ice-white body stuffed in the wall. It didn't work. "How—how did she die?" she asked. She thought of the earlier corpse, of Uyên's voice coolly telling her it was a woman called Lê Thị Hương Dinh. Dinh. Her friend, except that she'd come back from the dead only to die again in terrible pain.

"Stabbed," *Sunless Woods* said, in a cool voice. "Multiple times." And, after a pause, "It wasn't a pretty sight." It sounded like a reassurance, but her tone of voice belied it.

Vân looked at her hands, wondering what she could say. Laureate An Thành was there in her mind, offering quotes ranging from the flirtatious to the glib—nothing suitable or in good taste. "I thought it'd be treasure in the safe. Or a clue, like the one that led us to *The Elephant and Grass*." The Seven of Threads. As if on cue, Uyên's message popped up on her interface, with a helpful picture of the mạt chược tile—instead of the usual strings of copper coins of the suit, this one had actual threads, a delicate tracery of them with highlights picked in red, like the threads of fate. The red seemed to glisten like blood rather than good fortune.

Sunless Woods's voice was oddly gentle. "We all have secrets. Things we don't want to admit to."

Vân felt like she was choking. "I get it. You want to help me, but you can't do that if you don't know the truth."

A silence. Looking up, she found *Sunless Woods* sitting on her bed—and through the translucent mass of her avatar, she could see the stars, a spread of white, pulsing lights against the darkness of the sky—a vista that kept moving and changing, showing her the habitats of the Belt, and then more stars against the red and purple background of a distant nebula—and a persistent hum like a neverending song, the same one she'd heard in the asteroid field. "It doesn't work like that," *Sunless Woods* said. "You share with me what you're comfortable sharing. And I work around that. But I'd rather you didn't lie. Just tell me what things you don't want to talk about, and I won't inquire."

Bitter laughter choked her. "Like a true gentlewoman? You don't even know what I'm hiding."

A raised eyebrow. *Sunless Woods* closed her hand on hers— she must have shifted something in the overlays, because Vân could feel her, all of a sudden—and when she grabbed *Sunless Woods* back her fingers interlaced with cool, pliant skin whose touch sent a shiver through her spine. "No. What makes you think I would care?"

Again, bitter laughter. "Everyone does. They just like to say they don't."

Sunless Woods was silent. She was looking at Vân—not in the fond, amused way she'd had before, but with head cocked, her eyes with star-studded depths resting on Vân. Assessing her. Judging her. *Sunless Woods* hadn't withdrawn her hand, and Vân found herself clinging to it. "You think they'd cast you out, like the poetry club. Take your living from you and ensure you never found another. You've worked so hard at being where you are and you're afraid it would all collapse on a whim."

How did she know? How *could* she know? Vân felt exposed, in more ways than just the physical. "You—you take me here and shut me in this room, and give me Heaven knows what—"

"Medicine. You were at risk of contamination—"

"I'm not a child—I knew what I was getting into, and you know perfectly well we could have gone to any doctor in the Belt to get sorted out. But you take me here and take *everything* from me and then you have the nerve to say that you won't judge me, that I can keep my secrets! I'm *on* you! This room is

yours—all of it, all of *this*, this is your body, and you act like
I'm free—"

"You are." *Sunless Woods*'s voice was quiet. She let go of
Vân's hand, and stretched—and the stars stretched behind her
as if she were unrolling the canvas of the heavens, a shift that
spread over the entire room until they seemed once more to be
in Uyên's overlay, except that something was different about
this one—except that it wasn't just a poet's view of stars and
constellations, but the stars Vân had seen while she was out
there in the asteroid field, immobile pinpoints of light, and
over it all the harsh light of the sun glinting on the metal of a
ship's hull. "You're free here. Always. With nothing expected
or demanded. Not ever." She knelt then, wrapping her hands
around Vân's own—that diffuse warmth again, except it was
now pulsing like a living heart—and for a bare moment Vân,
feeling it travel through her bones like a pagoda bell, forgot
what it meant to breathe or sit—was hanging, weightless, in
the darkness of space, watching stars slowly wheel against the
light of the sun.

And then *Sunless Woods* withdrew her hands, and it felt as
though she'd just snuffed a candle out. "But I'm sorry if I gave
you a different impression. I had hoped—" she shook her head,
and the walls shifted to dark again. "Never mind. I'll have a
shuttle ready for you to get back to the habitat."

Vân expected her to merely disappear, but instead she
headed towards the door of the room—it irised open, revealing

the oily walls of a corridor with a painting of mountains shrouded in mist. Her body faded as she walked—by the time she was at the threshold she was nothing more than a faint outline, though the stars she had conjured remained in the room, faint dots of light. The noise she'd conjured—that soft, electric song of celestial bodies' radio waves—remained. A moment more, and she'd be gone altogether. She wouldn't be in the shuttle either, she'd just drop Vân off at the docks and walk out of her life. Or worse, keep this utterly professional, a favour from an elder to a younger, sorting out things that Vân wasn't mature or influential enough to do herself—all the while keeping that light, ironic distance she'd had before, in the poetry club.

Vân was up, almost before realizing she'd made the gesture. Her legs wobbled under her, threatening to collapse altogether. *Sunless Woods* hadn't seen her—or wasn't going back. The thought suddenly terrified her.

"Wait," she said. "Wait." Her voice felt raw and unused, as if she were speaking through a throat filleted by metal.

Sunless Woods paused—coalesced back into her avatar, one hand on the door as if to hold it open.

Vân said, "I'm sorry. I lost my temper."

A shrug. "And I lost my sense of boundaries." Her voice was sharp. "Flirting goes both ways."

"Flirting." The word was a stone dropped in a pond. "Is that what we're doing?"

Again, a carefully controlled shrug. *Sunless Woods* turned, to look at her. She wasn't human anymore: she was the ship, the immensity of a pitted hull seen from afar, the glint of light on fins and motors, the fluid gestures that weren't so much moving as diving through the air. Only a faint human outline remained—like a line that defined and constrained her at the same time. "If you want. Or we can investigate a murder."

Vân's chest hurt. She finally remembered to breathe. She said, slowly, carefully, "Remember that brawl I was a witness to, five years ago?"

A stillness, like a held breath. "Yes."

"It wasn't a brawl. It was my friends—Hương Lâm and Dinh, the people who lived with me. My…younger sisters. You can probably look them up on the network."

"In a heartbeat. But it's your story, not the network's."

"They—we were angry. At the scholars, at the wealthy, at all those given all the changes, all the honours, all the merit. We wanted to change the world. We wrote pamphlets and pro-tested and memorialised the magistrate, and all the things you get around to as drunk students." It was all coming out of her in a rush, words jumble with each other. "Except they went too far, and they got caught."

"Ah." *Sunless Woods*'s voice was flat. "A large enough theft to condemn them to death, or so you thought."

Vân wanted to say that theft was wrong; but Hương Lâm had stood by her, had encouraged her to build Laureate An

Thành, bringing rice wine to celebrate when Vân's patchwork of other people's ancestors finally came online—but Hương Lâm and Dinh had kept their silence for her sake, going into exile and never once breathing a word against Vân.

You could tell her about me. An Thành's voice was gentle.

Tell her, and be judged the way Uyên was going to judge her—castigated for turning the rules to her own advantage? "I saw what happened," she said. "They turned from barely tolerated to pariahs. Even before the trial, no one wanted to mention their names, or be associated with them in any fashion. And I—I just went along with it."

Sunless Woods was silent. Watching her. Weighing her.

Vân hesitated. In her thoughts, Laureate An Thành said nothing; was merely there, an inescapable reminder of good behaviour. "And they stood by me. I saw them, elder aunt. I—" she clamped her lips on the other pronoun that came to them, the more familiar, intimate one. "Dinh could barely walk. Hương Lâm had white scars on her arms—the marks of the militia's injectors, and she kept looking over her shoulders for something that wasn't there."

"They interrogated them."

"Of course. They had to get a confession, and make sure they had no accomplices. They could have dragged me down with them. Denounced me to make their own sentence lighter. I was eldest, and living with them. The weight of the law was against me."

"The law. A justice as clean and as meaningful as the blue of the sky." *Sunless Woods*'s voice was mirthless. "There's rather a dearth of blue over the habitats, isn't there."

Vân felt a familiar, almost deadened twist of fear in her chest. "You can't mean—"

Sunless Woods cocked her head. "That you were treated unfairly? I shouldn't have to say it to make it come true." Her voice sounded…tight, taut with something Vân couldn't name, as if at any moment the ship herself would burst and something else, something large and terrible was going to come out, a butterfly with bladed wings large enough to shred galaxies. She breathed in, slowly—or rather wanted it to be slow but felt only An Thành within her, and the depth of An Thành's own anger.

You can't think she's right. You're a scholar.

An Thành's voice was sharp. *You say this like it means merciless.*

Vân said, because she needed something, anything to paper over the chasm in the room, "They stood up for me."

"You think you owe them a debt? For being decent?" Vân couldn't read the emphasis *Sunless Woods* put on the words.

"For doing the right thing when I didn't? Yes," Vân said. "For—" words failed her, and she thought of every moment she'd believed them dead—grief and guilt and beneath it all, the relief they were no longer there, the same relief the orbitals had felt at being rid of thieves. "For everything I failed to do for them."

A silence. Laureate An Thành was quivering with anger in Vân's thoughts—Vân could only catch fragments of quotes, something about indigo and blue—the blue of fair justice, the indigo of righteous, irrevocable action which was also Vân's style name. And, in that silence, tightening like a silken noose, *Sunless Woods*'s sharp voice, "You're not the one who failed. And…regardless of what they did, back then, they haven't come back the same. Your friend—the dead one—"

"Dinh. Hương Dinh."

"Dinh killed that woman." *Sunless Woods*'s voice was cool. "Stuffed her in the safe to make sure she wouldn't be found, and then went to see Uyên."

Fear rose, choking her. "You can't mean—"

"You know exactly what I mean," *Sunless Woods* said. "And—" a pause, but it seemed to be more for effect than because she was looking for words—"It took two people to kill the woman in the safe."

Vân opened her mouth to say that Dinh Hương Lâm never would—and then realised that five years had passed, and her own friends were now as strangers to her. "Who was she?"

"The dead woman? One of Ngân Chi's poor relatives. They must have promised her whatever was inside the safe."

Except it had been empty, and the one in Uyên's quarters as well. "They're looking for wealth?"

Sunless Woods made a non-committal noise. "Yes. Whether it exists…that's another matter."

Vân was all too familiar with promises that never materialised. She tried to focus on what mattered. "Revenge." She couldn't imagine the sisters doing this, doing any of this; but thinking like this would only get Uyên killed. "They'll want Uyên."

"Yes." The ship was sitting next to her again, hands wrapped around hers, and Vân could feel *Sunless Woods*'s slow, steady heartbeat, the coolness of metal, with the faint warmth of motor oil trembling in the air. "The penalty doesn't get any worse for more murders unless we're talking relatives. It's slow death for them when they get caught. They'll have no incentive to stop. And I know you're concerned for Uyên, but consider this: you were there too, and they know who you are."

Vân opened her mouth to say they wouldn't have any interest in harming her, but the ship got there first.

"You're free and respected, and they're in immense pain and facing an agonising death whether they get caught or not. Don't underestimate what that does to people, please." The worst wasn't the words—it was the way she said them, the absolute certainty in them, the clear way *Sunless Woods* had already seen it.

"I'm not naive," Vân said.

"Of course not." The ship's smile was fond and sad. "You're merely trying to think the best of people, always. But I can't afford that if I want to protect you."

Protect.

We protected you, big'sis. Don't go and waste it all.

Vân tried to think of Hương Lâm—tried to think of facing her, of telling her everything Vân should have done—and saw only darkness where her friend's face had once been. "Hương Lâm and Dinh thought they were protecting me, too."

A silence, from the ship. "Yes." Her hands hadn't moved, but she raised Vân's own hands, brought them to her mouth. "I can't be them. I *wouldn't* be them, because I wouldn't make the choices they did. But I can make some of that fear you've been carrying for five years go away, if you'll let me."

Vân said, with a tongue that seemed to have melted into thick tar, "If I let you?"

Sunless Woods's smile was sharp and dazzling, and the entire room gathered itself behind it, illuminated, wounding. "If you let me care."

Her lips rested on the back of Vân's hands—she kissed them slowly, gently, a slow quivering shiver climbing through Vân's spine as she did so—she nudged Vân's thumbs into her mouth in a fluid, effortless movement, and then her lips were sucking on them with that same slow, steady rhythm, as inexorable as the wheeling of the stars in the sky. Vân clamped down on a moan, but *Sunless Woods*'s lips were still on her thumbs, every touch of them raw and unbearable and glorious, and her bots were flowing down Vân's back beneath the shirt, their legs trembling strokes on Vân's naked skin that seemed never to end—as though *Sunless Woods* were peeling away layers of skin and muscles until nothing remained but the shuddering mess at Vân's core.

Abruptly, it stopped. Vân, struggling to breathe through a chest that had contracted to burning breaths, tried to call the ship's name and only found incoherent, garbled syllables like warm embers in her mouth. *Sunless Woods*'s hands rested on her shoulders—Vân moved to grab them, to hold them closer to her chest and the knot of contorted desire there, but the ship's grip was iron. In her gaze, Vân saw the stars and the distant reflection of the Belt's habitats; and on her arms bots glinted, a match to the ones coiled in Vân's hair.

"You know I will stop," *Sunless Woods* said. Her voice was flat. "If you ask, if any point you feel this has gone too far—"

Laureate An Thành coalesced, briefly, into the desert of Vân's thoughts, reminding her of how the dance always went. "Yes," Vân said. "I can stop this with a word, and so can you." She drew *Sunless Woods* to her—feeling the heat and the weight of the ship on her arms, that body that was soft and pliant in a way no human body was—a touch relayed through layers of overlay that still set Vân's skin afire. "Don't you dare make decisions for me." Her bots came down her arms, flowing onto *Sunless Woods*'s own arms, until they nipped at the flesh of the neck—she hadn't been sure it'd work until the ship shuddered, and the entire room around them echoed this.

Vân fell with *Sunless Woods* on top of her—and saw the ship's avatar arch backwards, hair flowing oily and slick, her face planes of rugged metal reflecting starlight, her hands seeking Vân's chest, her bots delicately dancing on Vân's earlobes, pulling them again and again until the ache within her was too much and she moaned, over and over—and then there was nothing but the relentless heat of desire, whittling away at her whole being until she felt like an arrow finally loosed into space—going weightless and free into all-encompassing, comforting darkness.

VÂN WOKE UP. For a brief moment she didn't recognise where she was, and then she realised she was still in the same bed she'd been in before, except that she lay pillowed in the hollow of *Sunless Woods*'s shoulders, with the sound of distant starsong washing over her, and *Sunless Woods*'s bots curled up on her own shoulders and arms. Half of them scattered when she moved, and the ship beneath her stirred, the room slowly shifting into life in a word that Vân found hard to quantify—lights and oily reflections on metal becoming sharper and more in focus.

"Ship," she said, slowly, carefully. And then, the word itself tentative and presumptuous, sticking in her throat like the bone of a fish, "Big'sis." She started to ask what had happened, but it all came flooding back anyway, along with a memory of when she'd climaxed, her voice hoarse from moaning. "Hum. I—"

"Lil'sis," *Sunless Woods* said. Vân couldn't see her face, but she could feel the ship starting to pull away from her—the casual, arrogant mask being slipped back on. "Regrets?"

"No!" Vân fumbled for words. "I. Hum. It was amazing."
Laughter, good-humoured and sharp. "Yes. Same here."

Vân opened her mouth to say the ship had had other lovers, and then closed it when *Sunless Woods* ran a hand from the lobe of her ear down her cheek, slowly trailing beating warmth all the way down to her lips until she ached with need. "You're going to protest it can't possibly be that good. Please don't. Unless you want another demonstration of how much I enjoyed it?"

Vân wanted to, desperately—she nibbled on *Sunless Woods*'s fingers instead, inhaling her until the world seemed to tremble and fold around her hunger—and then letting go with a breath that felt torn out of her. "Later?"

A silence. Then *Sunless Woods* said, "You're worrying about what you told me."

Vân opened her mouth, and realised that wasn't it—that she didn't know what she felt anymore—a perverse mixture of relief that it had been said, that it was out in the open and not weighing her down anymore, and of fear that *Sunless Woods* would push harder, that she'd ask about An Thành and the secret that would get her kicked out of Uyên's house.

Sunless Woods rose, holding both of Vân's hands close to her—bringing them to her chest until all Vân could feel was the steady hum of motors. In her eyes, stars wheeled and slowly expanded, and sunlight glinted across the habitats spread like pearls against the blackness of space. "I have you," she said, simply. "I'm not in the habit of sharing confidences with other people."

Vân's voice choked in her chest. "You can't—"

"Love you? Care for you?"

"No, that's not what I meant. We—we barely know each other. We—" she sought for words. "We had amazing sex and that's really all there is…" Her voice trailed off, because she didn't know anymore what she'd say—what she'd be afraid to say, that the ship had seen dozens like her, that she was nothing special.

For a bare moment as they'd kissed—as *Sunless Woods*'s hands stroked her skin and the bots clung to her face, and everything felt tight and unbearably warm, taut with her desire—she'd been free, and it had changed everything— except that it couldn't last, it had never been meant to last.

An Thành whispered, *Love as lasting as the bamboo in winter, as sharp and as beautiful as frost on jade…*

As unattainable as nirvana, Vân said, more sharply than she'd meant to, and An Thành fell back, silenced.

Sunless Woods's voice was gentle, but as unbending as steel wrapped in silk. "And you think I'd leave you to fend off for yourself?"

"I—I don't know."

Laughter, gentle and amused. "As you say, you don't know me well. But I've never left someone in danger, and certainly not those I love." Her voice had hardened imperceptibly— she'd stretched, and she was…vast and terrible, the kind of ship whose passage scorched planets and moons. "I have people looking for Hương Lâm. The killing was a mistake. People won't want to get mixed up with her. We'll find her, and turn her in."

"You make it sound so simple."

"That's because it is." *Sunless Woods* was still holding Vân's hands against her chest: she bent over, and kissed Vân on the lips, gently, slowly. "Go home. You need to rest."

"You're cutting me out."

"No. I'm just making sure you get rest, and food." *Sunless Woods*'s voice went hard again. "And you're a gentle soul. Sometimes it's better not to know what I can get up to."

Vân said, before she could think, "You're not a scholar, are you."

A pause. She should have braced herself for harm; for the ship to eject her into space or silence her in so many other ways—but she couldn't. She couldn't imagine it, not from *Sunless Woods*.

The hands on hers squeezed, once, twice—and then *Sunless Woods* let go, and smiled at her, her avatar once more just an outline against the metal of the ship's body. "Firebrand. I'm the person who's made it her business to keep you and Uyên safe." Her voice was fond. "Ask me again, when this is over."

Vân swallowed the words she'd meant to say, and found only tightness in her chest, as if something long held was going to burst. "I will."

Sunless Woods laughed. "Good. Come on. Let's get you to a shuttle and back home."

ON HER WAY back, Vân saw the ship.

She was walking side by side with *Sunless Woods*'s avatar at first, and then she fell behind after the first couple corridors—as the holograms unfolded around her, unspooling ghostly dragons and fishermen, citadels of carved metal, and the distant sound of a flute mingled with the ever-present song of the stars. There was an octagonal room with a fountain—she couldn't tell if it was real or a hologram, the way the water sparkled with trapped starlight over a transparent floor, so that she was walking on the vastness of space, watching the curve of the outer habitats beneath her—and for a moment she hung again in space with the asteroids around her, where nothing mattered but the view unspooled around her, and the sound of her breath in the shadow-skin, and the slight, silent jolt of the glider as it accelerated. The corridors curved, sharply—their surfaces slick and oily, with just a hint of the deep spaces mindships went through—and opened up again at regular intervals into circular nooks whose walls were curio cabinets, their upper shelves showing tantalising hints of objects through latticework—from jade sculptures to jewellery to ancient scrolls, to sword sheaths and carved precious woods—to a fan of rice paper so thin and so brittle it had to be centuries old, with a poem written in the sweeping, evocative calligraphy of a master.

An Thành was keeping a silent catalogue of what she was seeing through the lattice—the jade lotus statues, the filigreed silver chests with patterns of peaches and deer, the rosewood stands adorned with precious rocks. When she got to the fan she paused, and if she'd been incarnate her breath would have caught in her chest. *That's pre exodus. From Old Earth. Or a very good replica.*

Which made it almost the same worth as the original—it wasn't the age, but the time that had gone into recreating it that created the value. This was almost—but not quite—the treasure trove of a wealthy scholar, the life Vân occasionally dreamt of as an unattainable fancy, except for a few wrong notes.

You're not a scholar, are you.

Ask me again after this.

There were more cabinets and more treasures, and bookshelves faintly shimmering into existence, loaded with scrolls from romantic space opera to martial heroes, and the faint sound of water answering the plaintive starsong. The ship was by her side again, holding her hand, her touch warm and comforting—and her bots had spread around them both in a teardrop shape, their legs faintly clicking on the floor.

Vân found her voice. "You're flirting with me."

"Is that what I'm doing?" *Sunless Woods* smiled. "I was rather thinking I'd sweep you off your feet." And ran a hand on Vân's hair, softly stroking the topknot open, fingers gently running on Vân's scalp, a slow steady combing even as *Sunless Woods* bore her against the corridor's wall and held her there.

Vân scrabbled, fingers finding *Sunless Woods*'s back, and the stream of bots there—her hands dancing over them as if she were playing on silk strings—*Sunless Woods*'s lips clamped on a moan that twisted the corridor out of shape, while behind Vân the wall yielded like living skin, holding her tight in an endless embrace, and everything stellated into that craved sense of release.

AFTERWARDS, THEY SAT side by side, holding hands on the shuttle. Vân felt held by more than hands—by the bench and by the walls, by the shuttle itself, wrapped and cocooned in *Sunless Woods*'s embrace. No words would come; for a while she did nothing but lay back against the shuttle's wall, feeling the ship's heartbeat against her own body.

"I'll send someone," *Sunless Woods* said. "To keep an eye on you and Uyên."

Vân opened her mouth to protest, but An Thành got there first.

This isn't the time for pride or principles, An Thành said, severely. *Take the help offered.*

Vân started to protest principles weren't optional, and then she thought of Uyên. "Of course," she said. "Thank you, big'sis."

"Of course." *Sunless Woods* smiled. "Now go home and rest. I'll see you later."

They kissed, on the docks—and Vân walked home with the taste of motor oil and starlight in her mouth.

SUNLESS WOODS HADN'T meant to lie to Vân.

Rather, to put things in the proper order, she hadn't meant to sleep with Vân in the first place—except that she'd seen that bruised, wounded expression on Vân's face, the way it had deepened as she'd told her story—and *Sunless Woods* was too old, too observant not to see the parts where Vân stopped, where she censured herself, where she was still afraid. She'd felt the way the hands in hers had tightened, seen the tenseness in Vân's shoulders and back—a dam ready to burst, and nothing behind it but fear and guilt—and something in her had shifted, like something breaking in her own heartroom.

The second time…ah well, for the second time she didn't have a convenient excuse, other than it had been slow and as hot as the hearts of stars and in all ways magnificent.

You're not a scholar, are you. She hadn't meant to reveal herself, either; or more of herself than she'd ever shown any of her precious flirts. She should have done what she'd always done: stick to the identity she was impersonating, and have quick, pleasurable sex that they could both look back on fondly—and then leaving or breaking it off before it had any chance to change.

Except that Vân was…all seriousness and integrity, with a sense of duty the size of planets—and all of it should have made *Sunless Woods* run away very fast, but instead it kept dragging her back in no matter how much she tried to pull away. She'd never seen anyone quite like Vân—and she thought that sleeping with her would solve the problem, at least, of the novelty.

It had; and it had spectacularly failed to solve her other problems.

She pinged *Wine* through the network, asking the other ship if she could spare either herself or a crew member to watch over Vân. *Wine* answered with her customary sparseness, saying she was at loose ends in any case, though *Sunless Woods* didn't believe her for one moment. *Wine* had liked Vân.

Wine was smart enough to not make comments about *Sunless Woods*'s love life, which just left *Sunless Woods* with no one to blame but herself.

She really hadn't meant to lie to Vân, but she had. She'd told Vân she wasn't cutting her out, but the truth was that she'd surrender herself and all her treasures to the militia before taking Vân along to hunt down a band of thieves who'd murdered a woman and stuffed her in a safe—not only that, but former friends of Vân with every reason to bear her a grudge. Whatever Vân seemed to think of Hương Lâm, *Sunless Woods* wasn't taken in: this was thieves who'd turned to murder on their way to the money of their dreams, and they wouldn't stop just for the sake of old friendships, and that went double when one of them had already died for said money.

Which meant she had to get them out of Vân's life, and fast.

She stood, for a while, in front of the curio cabinets that had so entranced Vân—not her scholar's treasures but the gains of a lifetime of thefts, the fan Thiên Hoa had poached from the Purple Forbidden City on the First Planet, the unobtrusive jade dragon that was a carving from Quý Xuân that looked as though it was leaping to the stars. She held it in her hand, feeling the coolness of stone give way to pulsing warmth—everything she'd taken against all odds, and the time she and Hải's children had led a desperate rescue to free Thiên Hoa from jail before she could be sentenced to branding or penal servitude.

She had done it before, and she could do it again.

She called Thiên Hoa.

"Big'sis." The other woman was walking in the common spaces of a habitat *Sunless Woods* couldn't identify—a brief pause and then it updated, showing her in Pure Metal Quarter in the Sword Turtle habitat, a district filled with teahouses and restaurants catering to the less savoury people on the social scale.

"Tell me you have something," *Sunless Woods* said.

"Ah." Thiên Hoa was silent, for a while, looking at *Sunless Woods*'s avatar. That mood, her eyes said. The harsh, implacable ship coming down like the wrath of heaven and earth. "That bad?"

"I have this pressing need to make someone very uncomfortable until they leave Vân and Uyên's life."

"Ah," Thiên Hoa said again. "Come down with me, will you?"

Shipminds didn't need to take shuttles, or make flight plans. *Sunless Woods* fielded in a query with the Mind of the habitat—which was accepted with a matter of course, her avatar allowed to incarnate in the corridors. She called up the bots she had in reserve on every habitat, and met Thiên Hoa in front of a street seller offering meat skewers with a tantalizing smell of scorched lemongrass and fish sauce.

"I have a lead," Thiên Hoa said, curtly nodding to *Sunless Woods* as she arrived. She was nibbling at a skewer, and handed its overlay version to *Sunless Woods*. As *Sunless Woods* consumed it she got a brief, haunting memory of a meal in the communal kitchen with Mother and her long-dead siblings fighting for meat. Thiên Hoa shared, briefly, footage from the habitat: Ái Hồng sharing tea and talking with animation to a couple of strangers. Neither of them was Dinh, but the eldest among them—tall, regal and with the no-nonsense air of someone who wasn't used to being contradicted—had a faint family resemblance to her. Hương Lâm, probably: strange how even with the physical and genetic alterations they ended up so close to each other.

"One week ago," *Sunless Woods* said, noticing the time stamp. *"Tea on White Sands."* It was a teahouse on the outer rings of the habitat. "I'm not sure—"

Thiên Hoa smiled. "So the interesting thing about this is that it's the last footage of Ái Hồng I find anywhere. The next thing she does is board a shuttle at the docks with a flight plan for the asteroids around *The Elephant and Grass.*" She tapped the skewers against her cheek, heedless of the streak of sauce it left on her skin. More footage, a little less distinct—she wouldn't have been able to make out the faces but now that she'd seen them from closer in the bar, the gait and postures of two of them were unmistakable.

Sunless Woods thought, fast—which wasn't hard, as she could run sixteen parallel threads before she markedly slowed down. "All right, so we know what they look like. I presume you tracked them using other footage from other areas."

"Eeh, other areas is hard," Thiên Hoa said. "They don't keep archives for long enough. Private shops, though… It's amazing how much archiving the shady teahouses keep, just in case one of their shadier customers decides to cross the line and they need hard evidence for blackmail." A wide smile. "And amazing how little encryption they put on said archives. Like a knife through ripe mango cheeks."

"You're not going to make me believe you just found out about this."

An innocent smile from Thiên Hoa. "Honest merchant, remember? Anyway, I have one of them right now. *The Cups of Hollow Bamboo.*"

"Uh." It was the teahouse across the plaza, which looked like a haunt of middle-class scholars and merchants. The footage Thiên Hoa sent showed the woman—not Hương Lâm, the other one—sitting down with what looked to be a merchant wearing pale orange robes, his face creased in thought. *Sunless Woods* got to work on the audio on a background thread, separating it from the rest of the ambient sound. It was live.

"They're going to be sitting down for a bit," Thiên Hoa said, but *Sunless Woods*'s cleaning algorithms came up with words of the conversation.

"Passage beyond…price…soon."

"They're negotiating for a spaceship. Probably beyond the Đại Việt Empire."

Thiên Hoa's face went flat. "What kind of timeline?"

"A few days."

"Then they haven't scored yet, but there's no time to waste. All right then."

And, without another word, she dropped the skewer, and marched across the street.

Sunless Woods weighed the chances of the Mind's habitat granting her teleportation. She'd have to provide a good reason to disrupt the physicality imposed on the habitat, and that would make her stand out. Never mind. She altered the posture of her avatar slightly, to seem more human, and with the mannerisms and bearing of a higher-class scholar, one who most *definitely* wouldn't ordinarily patronise the teahouse.

Inside, Thiên Hoa had finished arguing with the waiter at the entrance: by the looks of it, paying a bribe to let herself in without taking a table. The waiter took one look at *Sunless Woods* and the determined way she was marching in, and bowed himself out of the way.

The common tables held no one matching the video: Thiên Hoa was now moving through the scattered private booths with a faint look of concentration, hacking into privacy screen after privacy screen to see inside the darkened overlay walls. *Sunless Woods* called up her bots, and scattered them—except that she was struggling to get them authorisation to breach private overlays, the habitat's Mind being justifiably peeved at demands that didn't stem from maintenance needs.

Here, Thiên Hoa said, and sent through her own authorisations. A dozen, a hundred simultaneous feeds rising in *Sunless Woods*'s awareness—and all the threads of her thoughts engaged at the same time, sorting out the accumulated information until she found what she was looking for, while her avatar stood motionless in the middle of the floor, every pretence of humanity stripped from it, and the stars beneath

Sunless Woods's ship body spreading under its feet, across the floor of the teahouse.

There.

They were in one of the isolated booths at the very end of the room, just a few forelengths away from the back door of the teahouse. She pinged Thiên Hoa with the location, but Thiên Hoa was already moving—and the woman and the merchant were both rising, running towards the door.

No feeds outside, or the really bad communal ones: they'd lose them if they went too far outside the teahouse.

There was no time.

Sunless Woods couldn't teleport, but she could tweak a few things—namely, the length of her strides and the speed of her leg movements. She didn't run so much as glided—gathering back to herself the images of the stars as she compressed everything into her avatar and the handful of bots close enough to the booth—two groups of them went for the woman's legs, but the woman's own bots flowed down to meet them, heading them off.

Thiên Hoa was arguing with the merchant, who wouldn't get out of her way and whose face was flustered in the familiar outrage. If *Sunless Woods* had been paying attention she would have picked up their conversation, but all her attention was on the woman: the merchant was just a random bystander who happened to have berths free on a spaceship.

The woman threw up the privacy screen to maximum opacity, suddenly vanishing from *Sunless Woods*'s field of view.

Sunless Woods cursed—she should have expected this, and she couldn't just turn off the overlay because the woman had priority access to it by virtue of the authorisations conferred on her by the teahouse.

The door. She was going to move towards the door. *Sunless Woods* sent queries to the teahouse and the habitat's Mind, in the forlorn hope either of them would be granted in time, and ran towards where she remembered the door was.

It wasn't there. The privacy screen obscured it, and muffled all sounds so that all that floated to her was the argument Thiên Hoa was having with the merchant. By Thiên Hoa's face, she was looking for a good excuse to knock the merchant flat, except that they had enough trouble with one fugitive without adding a fight with the wrong person into the mix. Could *Sunless Woods* get a bot with a sedative-loaded injector on the merchant's neck? Probably not: the merchant had bots of his own.

Ah-ha. The teahouse had finally granted her access to the privacy screen on the basis of her location, though her access remained limited. *Sunless Woods* threw all she had at the privacy screen: it wobbled and went semi-transparent, enough to see that the woman was nowhere behind it.

Where—

The door was closed, and her bots' sensors hadn't heard it move. Perhaps she'd hacked it in a way that wouldn't show up?

Her gut feeling was that she hadn't. Which meant she had to be elsewhere.

Where—

Movement, on *Sunless Woods*'s right, behind another privacy screen. She gave up on querying the teahouse, and instead moved all her bots towards it, running enhancing algorithms to fuse the bots' minute perceptions into hers. A wall of chittering noise that was the privacy screen's muffling—a sharp, unpleasant noise that seemed to take over everything, and the same across her field of vision, something like dirty, dead snow rising to fill the space where the table should have been.

But, in that space, there was movement. It was faint and barely perceptible, but she was good at making that out—and the bots latched onto it, amplifying it even as her algorithms adapted to filter out the rest of the noise. A vague shape—no, four vague shapes, but only one of them was running, the other three were just barely rising from the table they'd been sitting at.

Sunless Woods sent half of her bots towards it, and moved to the other side of the privacy screen. From her bots came the indistinct, blurred images and sounds of other bots getting in their way—but, as the woman exited the zone of the privacy screen with barely a glance behind her, *Sunless Woods* was already there—and behind her Thiên Hoa, still peevish-looking from her argument with the merchant.

The woman—out of breath, her topknot in disarray, her bots still struggling to free themselves from *Sunless Woods*'s bots—hesitated, her eyes darting left and right as if there was any chance of escape, but there was nothing, and none of the teahouse's customers or staff were going to get embroiled with what obviously looked like a private, nasty but localised affair.

They had her.

Sunless Woods smiled, slow and revealing rows of pearlescent teeth around a black and vast maw. "Going somewhere?"

THE WOMAN SAT in a high-backed chair in one of the private rooms of the teahouse, unmoving—body restrained by ropes, and by *Sunless Woods*'s bots on her chest, ankles and wrists, monitoring her for the slightest move.

Thiên Hoa had smoothed out everything with the teahouse, while *Sunless Woods* stood looking forbidding and pretending to be a much higher-ranked scholar than she currently was. The privacy screen was set to muffle all sounds, and the walls of the room themselves were padded—which suggested they weren't the first set of customers to need a room for questionable purposes, and in turn that the teahouse was much less respectable than it advertised.

Not that *Sunless Woods* was surprised. The scholars were quick to ascertain their natural merit in the order of things, but they could be as arrogant and as rotten as any of the lowlifes they derided.

She looked up as Thiên Hoa and *Sunless Woods* walked into the room, *Sunless Woods* matching the rhythm of her own steps perfectly to Thiên Hoa—her reaction times, even with the lag, were faster than humans', and she knew how disturbing this could be on a primal level.

"So," Thiên Hoa said. She had a vacuum knife in her hands—not turned on, but the woman's gaze went to it nevertheless. "I did a little digging. Your name is Hoàng Thị Lam Khê. You hire yourself out as bodyguard, with a variety of less savoury and less legal occupations that I don't have time to go into but that I'm sure will interest the militia very much."

The woman blinked. It was minute, but matched by a slight speeding up of her heart rate. *Sunless Woods* said, "Mind you, I'm pretty sure they won't have to dig very far for things of interest. Murder is the slow death, isn't it?"

She and Thiên Hoa had never killed anyone, but it didn't mean they couldn't rough Khê up both mentally and physically. *Wine*, ever the philosopher, would probably argue that by turning Khê over to the militia, they'd be responsible for her death. *Sunless Woods* thought Khê had gotten everything she'd ever asked for when she and her friends had made the decision to stab Ái Hồng to death.

"I don't know what you mean," Khê said.

"Oh, don't give me that." *Sunless Woods* materialized her own vacuum knife—which wouldn't cut anything unless she brute forced her way through the woman's physical access layers, but she didn't need to do any of that, because Thiên Hoa was an effective threat of all her own. "I found the body. And

I'm not amused—" she leaned in a fraction—"that you're going sowing chaos in my territory." She used an ambiguous word that meant the place she lived in, but also the stretch of station space a gang would call theirs—a very fine line to walk, because she didn't want to blow her cover.

Khê stared at her, levelly.

"Don't give me that either," *Sunless Woods* said. "I have more sensitive bots than yours. You're scared. Talk. Who are they, and what are they looking for?"

"Why should I bother?" Khê's voice was soft.

Thiên Hoa leaned over, her mannerisms changing slightly to become the lowborn ones rather than the wealthy First Planet ones she'd affected. "They hired you, didn't they? Blood's on their hands, not yours."

"Makes no difference," Khê said. She sounded almost regretful.

Thiên Hoa looked at *Sunless Woods*, and sent her a subvocalised message.

Let me deal with it.

Going to sympathize with her?

You know what I'm going to offer her, Thiên Hoa said. She was looking at Khê, thoughtfully.

Legal help, or escaping the militia, or both. Which meant she'd never see the punishment for her crime.

Thiên Hoa said, *You have to figure out what you want. Can't have everything.*

Sunless Woods weighed it up. Khê was scared, but they couldn't use that fear against her, because the militia would indict her for murder and inflict the slow death on her. And they needed to find Hương Lâm to keep Vân safe.

She wanted to be in charge and mete rough justice and keep Vân safe, but Thiên Hoa was right: she couldn't have both of these.

All yours, she said, grudgingly.

SUNLESS WOODS WAS leaning against the corridor of the teahouse when Thiên Hoa came out. She was sipping on a cup of tea that was neither as good nor as evocative as the ones Vân had served her, which only increased her annoyance.

"So?" she asked.

Thiên Hoa shrugged. "You're not going to like it."

Sunless Woods was no longer in the mood for games, and especially not Thiên Hoa's borderline sadistic varieties. "Do you know where Hương Lâm is?"

"Yes."

"Then that's all I need to know."

Thiên Hoa's hand on her shoulder stopped her—not quite physically, but a faint thing almost indistinguishable from a breath of wind in the corridor. "Ái Hồng died because there was no fortune. Because Ngân Chi gambled it away before she died. Because the safe in Uyên's room was the last such place to try, and because Hương Lâm already knew it would be empty."

"Dinh tried to get to it," *Sunless Woods* said.

"Yes. Dinh was in pain and desperate. If Hương Lâm had had her way, she'd never have gone."

"I fail to see what any of this has to do with Vân," *Sunless Woods* said, except that of course there was no treasure, no fortune, nothing that she could give Vân to make it all worth it. She hadn't thought disappointment could be a physical thing—as if some giant hand were twisting her hull out of shape, and she could barely hold in the pain.

Thiên Hoa smiled. "That's because you were right. They *are* about to score."

"On a non-existent fortune?"

"I didn't say that." Thiên Hoa's smile was wide and wicked. "They have another target. Another treasure of great value. You'll like this."

Sunless Woods had had enough of being jerked around—not that she didn't love Thiên Hoa, but there were limits. "Not really, no. Another treasure that's smaller and more attainable, and that they'll find in someone's home? I'd rather hoped—"

"No no no." Thiên Hoa waggled a finger. Her face had grown stern and distant again: the ancestor in the mem-implant, advising her to rephrase what she'd been saying. "Fine, fine," she said, somewhat impatiently to her ghostly ancestor. And, to *Sunless Woods*, "You're thinking too much like a thief."

"I was under the impression I was one."

"Yes, but—" Thiên Hoa waved a hand, again. "You're thinking 'great value' as in the penal code. The threshold of stolen goods that changes the sentence from exile from the Empire to lifelong servitude or death."

"And I should be thinking of…?"

Thiên Hoa's eyes glittered. "Legends. The kind of wealth found in jade-and-emerald citadels, or in dragon kingdoms. The way Khê spoke of it, it was the kind of theft that'd go down in historians' records."

Fame. Not just the endless march of news channels wondering how she had done it at all, but the kind that'd go enshrined in the official histories, taught in schools—a giant mocking gesture to the Empire that had turned its back on them. A splash big enough to keep her in the limelight for years, and a fortune for Vân and Uyên, something honestly gotten rather than the inacceptable awkwardness of *Sunless Woods* forcing stolen money on them…

Something was hardening in *Sunless Woods*'s gut, a mixture of worry for Vân and anger at Hương Lâm, and at herself for being out of the game for so long, for allowing herself to sink into obscurity, to be turned into so much lesser than she was—she'd show Vân, she'd show them all that she wasn't to be trifled with.

"A legend," she said, sharply. "That will do quite nicely. Come on, lil'sis. Let's go pay our respects to Hương Lâm."

VÂN GOT HOME, and found *The Bearer of Healing Wine, Sunless Woods*'s mindship friend, waiting for her. "Big'sis," she said, bowing, and the ship laughed.

"That's not quite what I had in mind when I told you to get less familiar."

In their common quarters, Uyên was sitting in front of a calligraphy exercise with the nervous, pent-up energy that suggested anything would send her careening down a new train of thought. She fairly jumped up when she saw Vân. "Teacher!"

Wine had followed Vân into the room. Uyên frowned when she saw her—but then she must have checked the label in the network and realised *Wine* wasn't another avatar of *Sunless Woods*.

"She's a friend." Vân didn't want to say bodyguard, because Uyên would have too many questions. "She's come to help with some questions I had on books."

Uyên made a face. "Please tell me we're not about to have a lesson. Not now."

Vân knew Uyên wouldn't be able to sit still for it, at least not until she got the curiosity out of the way. She summarised, quickly, what had happened onboard the dead ship, carefully leaving out any mention of the aftermath. Nevertheless, she could tell Uyên wasn't convinced.

"Uh," Uyên said when Vân was done. "Murder."

"I don't think they have any interest in you anymore," *Wine* said. "They'll be trying to shake off *Sunless Woods*'s pursuit." It was very clearly a lie, but apparently enough gravitas from an authority figure was enough to convince Uyên.

Or, to be more accurate: Uyên had other preoccupations. "So *Sunless Woods* is really digging into this. She sounds pretty…driven."

Vân tried not to blush, but it was futile. Uyên's smile was broad.

"She's nice," Vân said, non-committal.

Wine made a sound that sounded suspiciously like choked laughter, but mercifully didn't take it further. Vân wanted to disappear into the floor. "So," the ship said, "any place where I can set up and work?"

They ended up giving her some space in Uyên's larger quarters, where she unpacked a simulation of what looked like bot parts and settled down to watch them with the intentness of a monk meditating on the secrets of the universe.

"So," Uyên said casually—too casually—"what she was saying about *Sunless Woods* sorting that out—"

Vân breathed in, sharply, thinking of Hương Lâm's face, of the hardness in *Sunless Woods*'s voice when she said the problem was as good as dealt with—of what it meant, of who the ship really was—"I believe her," she said, and her heart felt it was going to burst out of her chest—as if she'd been running in blind panic through darkness from something fanged and clawed.

"Ah." Uyên's gaze was uncomfortably sharp.

"Come on," Vân said. "Let's talk about Quý Xuân and her poetry."

She taught it on automatic, An Thành interjecting with allusions and the commentary of other scholars—the different interpretations and their weight, and how it called back to earlier poets from before the Exodus. It should have been comforting—she should have been feeling An Thành's presence in her thoughts like the weight of a shadow-skin in vacuum, the knowledge that someone would be there to catch her if she faltered in her scholarship—but instead all she could see was Uyên's gaze, the weight of it, the obvious admiration in her eyes—everything that had once made her happy and was now shrivelled by the knowledge of how close she was to losing it all—how Uyên would never forgive her for An Thành or any of the secrets she was keeping as her duty—and the ship and the paintings and lying on *Sunless Woods*'s chest with the song of the stars in her ears—and how she didn't know where she stood with her or what any of it meant.

An Thành said, *Truth uttered before its time is always dangerous, but sincerity is always the way of Heaven.*

No, Vân said. *You're wrong. You're wrong.*

She couldn't breathe, anymore.

"Teacher? Is anything wrong?"

"I'm fine," Vân said. "Why don't you write some commentary on Quý Xuân yourself? I'll come back and check up on you."

Uyên threw her a sharp glance but didn't protest.

In her quarters, everything was smaller and suffocating, and she couldn't seem to lie down and relax. A blinking light caught her attention: a message that had lain in her queue for a while. She opened it before she could think: a hologram coalesced in the middle of her bedroom.

It was the Seven of Threads.

The exact same design Uyên had found, a stylised painting on the tile with the individual threads of the strings glistening in the light—and behind were the other ones, the Seven of Infinities, the mathematical symbol drawn in ink as black as ebony, with a faint scattering of stars over the strokes; the Seven of Barrels, the circles enclosing a glistening liquid that might have been wine or oil, with translucent, shadowy reflections on their surface like the faces of demons or ghosts.

Then they both faded, and she saw Hương Lâm's face staring at her.

It was her: not the face she currently wore—because she and Dinh had altered themselves so thoroughly in order to be able to come back to the Belt—but a skillful overlay that mimicked the movements of her gen-modded features, simulating the person Vân had once known.

"Elder sister. We need to talk. Please." Her voice was raw and exhausted, and even the overlay couldn't disguise the shadow of pain and fear in her eyes.

Vân opened her mouth. Words crowded behind it: everything that *Sunless Woods* had warned her about, how much Hương Lâm would want to hurt her—but nothing would come out.

"I—" Hương Lâm swallowed. "I didn't mean for things to turn out that way. It…" she stopped then, looking for words—she looked small and defeated and in immense pain, and Vân felt her own unsaid words like cold stones in her throat. "It all went wrong, didn't it? Please, elder sister. I trust you." She faded away, and the hologram became a set of coordinates somewhere in the outer rings of the habitat.

Elder sister.

Vân's hands hurt: she unclenched them, realising her nails had dug into her skin hard enough to break it. Blood beaded within her palm: her own bots came to staunch the wound, and still she couldn't bring herself to move.

I trust you.

She'd trusted Vân, once: to keep her mouth shut, to let Hương Lâm and Dinh sacrifice themselves and remain silent herself, to let them die rather than be implicated.

The smart, sensible thing would have been to tell *Sunless Woods;* to sit back and let it all happen, the chase, the militia arrest—and then she remembered the harshness of *Sunless*

Woods's voice, and that murder was the slow death—a flash of a body stretched on a rack, and executioners' bots slowly slicing away bits of flesh, and blood falling drop by drop on polished metal.

Laureate? she asked, and within her An Thành, startled, stirred.

The one who steals salt dies of thirst unless debts are repaid, An Thành said, and her voice was almost gentle.

Please, elder sister.

She'd failed them once, and Dinh had died in terrible agony—and would she really fail them a second time?

SNEAKING OUT WAS surprisingly easy. *Wine* was setting up surveillance devices and chatting to a concerned Uyên, and was focusing on problems coming from outside rather than people under her charge leaving. Vân caught scraps of their conversation as she came out: "wound tight…she needs to rest…a shock."

They were concerned about her—which might have stopped her in other circumstances.

The address Hương Lâm had given her was in the Six Families district, on the outskirts of the habitat. As she moved away from the central districts, the overlays got more and more lurid and elaborate to disguise the rundown structures, the corridors where the paint was flaking and dull. And then there were no overlays at all, just metal so roughly polished it looked pitted, people's personal bots rather than the habitat ones painting over the blank walls, and doors that only fitted into their frame because they'd been melted and twisted into shape.

The address Hương Lâm had given her was one of those doors. It bulged outwards, and someone had painted a sprig of apricot flowers that had got torn in half when the metal piece was cut. The faint sheen on the metal reminded her, for a moment, of *Sunless Woods*'s hull, and she had to breathe slowly and quietly before she could knock, punching in the code that Hương Lâm had given her.

The door didn't so much swing open as collapse inwards with a shriek. Inside was only darkness. "Younger sister? It's me."

"In here," a distant voice said.

Vân's heart beat so strongly she felt it was going to burst through her chest. She walked forward, and the darkness engulfed her—the air felt stale, and with that rancid aftertaste of not passing through enough purifiers. Almost as if she were back in space, except that there was nothing ahead of her but the price for her own foolish mistakes.

An Thành was silent within her: Vân could feel the mem-implant's wary watchfulness, but of course she'd never been meant to judge anything.

Sunless Woods *would judge*, a small, treacherous voice said, within Vân. Sunless Woods *would care*.

Vân shushed it.

The corridor opened on a space that was almost obscenely wide: a former teahouse, except that the profusion of tables were gone, and only a single one remained in the centre of the room. There were no overlays. No, that wasn't true. For as Vân went deeper into the room, towards the waiting figure of Hương Lâm behind the table, something shimmered into existence under her feet: mạt chược tiles, the same ones drawn by Dinh, the brushstrokes of the Infinities, the Barrels and their glistening contents, the Threads, sharply delineated—and the other tiles too; the replacement tiles with their coloured, sweeping calligraphy, the flowers scattered across the pristine white of the tiles; the winds, represented not as words or characters, but as serpentine shapes stretching towards the top of the tiles, with the patterns of nebulas on their scales…

"Elder sister." Hương Lâm looked up from the table, where three cups of steaming tea waited for Vân. "I hadn't expected you to come." She sounded exhausted and hurt: the face she was wearing was the new one, but her mannerisms and voice had barely changed. They could almost have been back five years ago, in that faraway lifetime before the thefts, before the militia. Behind Hương Lâm was the Seven of Infinities, slowly morphing into the other two Seven tiles.

Vân pulled out the chair and sat. In her thoughts was only silence, with even Laureate An Thành at a loss for words. "I had to," she said, because nothing but the truth was left. She saw that the third cup was merely a hologram, much like the ones on the ancestral altars. "Dinh…"

"I can't speak about her. Not now." Hương Lâm inhaled, sharply. "Here. Have your tea."

It wasn't an overlay, but something with a faint, acrid taste of grass that burnt all the way down into the nauseous emptiness of Vân's belly. Hương Lâm sipped hers, grimacing—watching Vân intently.

Vân said, finally, "I've always thought you were dead," which was trite but needed to be said.

"We might as well have been." Hương Lâm moved slowly, carefully, as if her body were made of glass—and Vân remembered what *Wine* had said about Dinh, the constant agony she'd been in that had finally killed her. "Exiled beyond the Belt and beyond the numbered planets. It's the places no one wants to go to, the fire-scorched lands, the atmospheres that can't be breathed." Her breath was slow and ragged. "We were on Hoả Giả Sơn Tinh. It's mostly lava and sulphur, and one dome. If you want to go out, you need an expensive suit that exiles like us can't afford. We couldn't get work, because no one would hire us. We couldn't contact anyone, because the network was local, and everything else needed to be sent through the government array. That's more money you didn't have."

"I should have sent you some."

"Why would you? You thought we were dead."

"I had no idea."

"I know you didn't." Hương Lâm's face twisted. "I'm not here to reproach you. You did what you had to. You kept your silence, and look at you." She sounded fond. "You have a post. You have success, although you could have gone so much higher."

Vân thought, uncomfortably, of her discussion with Uyên. "I don't want to go higher. I'm happy here." Why did the second sentence sound like a lie? "Why are you here, younger sister?" And, because she had to, "People died. Not just Dinh."

Hương Lâm exhaled. She stared at her tea for a while, while the bots on her shoulders descended to fetch more leaves. "We didn't have a choice. You have to understand. What it's like to not be condemned to death, but to slowly choke. To be exiled. To be marked. To be cut off from our families, from society. From everything that matters. We might as well have been dead: it would have been kinder, even the slow death."

"I'm sorry," Vân said, and it sounded small and inadequate. But another, irrepressible thought came right afterward—one An Thành silently nodded in acquiescence to: "You killed Ái Hồng. Everything that happened to you cannot be an excuse."

Bitter laughter, from Hương Lâm. She reached into her sleeves, and set a single tile on the table: one of the Four Noble Professions, the Scholar: a silhouette holding a brush and an inkstone, the background adorned with a single hollow bamboo under the moon, Dinh's forceful drawing, shadowed and sinister, laying bare the pain that had killed her, the pain that was tearing Hương Lâm apart. "That's you all over, isn't it. Refusing to understand how things truly work. How dark it can get."

"I'm no stranger to darkness."

"You're sheltered."

"Because you sheltered me?"

"Is that not the way it happened?" Hương Lâm smiled, and for a bare moment Vân saw, beneath the overlay, the tautness of the face, the creases of agonising pain, and her heart, stretched thin and desperate, broke.

"Please," she said. "Please stop. I know I wasn't there for you, but this can't go on. You have to see there's only one ending to all of this. If you turn yourself in, they'll be merciful."

"A reduction of one degree? From agonising death to being sent painlessly into Hell?"

"Please." Vân's hands were shaking. The teacup wobbled in her grasp—she tried to put it back on the table, and something went wrong and sent it crashing to the floor. Hương Lâm barely glanced at it as her bots gathered to pick up the shards. "I'm sorry," Vân said. "I should have said something. I would have sent you money—I should have sent you money—but it's too late." She'd prospered while they suffered; had let the debt she owed them grow as large and heavy as a banyan tree. But it had all been an impossible, ephemeral dream.

"Is it?" Hương Lâm's eyes glinted in the darkness. She set down her own teacup, and a wave of incontrollable nausea racked Vân from head to toe. "You can't pay, elder sister. You genuinely can't. If you were an official—if you'd sat for the exams and been posted as a magistrate, if you'd entered the Brush Forest Academy, then perhaps you'd have a fortune to spend."

"You don't need a fortune," Vân said, chilled. Every word felt like weighted stones: even shaping her mouth around them exhausted her.

"I *deserve* a fortune."

"Ngân Chi…"

"Ngân Chi never had one. But fortunately, you still do."

The room was growing dark, and warm, unbearably so: Vân tried to rise, but found that her legs wouldn't obey her—her hands, scrabbling to hold the arms of the chair, except that nothing would move, and something as vast and tenebrous as the abyss of space opened beneath her, only waiting to drag her in.

Hương Lâm said, matter-of-factly, "You made a mem-implant. You *created* an ancestor. Don't you understand?"

An Thành—she could feel An Thành in her mind, could feel her steely disapproval of Hương Lâm and all she stood for, but it was as if she were behind a pane of glass.

The bots brought back the shards of the teacup, laid them on the table. Something glistened there, too dark and too thick to be tea dregs—and the room spun and spun and wouldn't stop, and Vân finally understood why she was there, that it had never been about begging for her help or her forgiveness, but for something far darker—as *Sunless Woods* had said, why would Hương Lâm stop, when she would die anyway?

Hương Lâm said, "Getting someone else's ancestral implants is risky and uncertain, but you created a personality with no blood attachments. A fiction of the perfect scholar, with knowledge far exceeding those of anyone who ever lived. A treasure beyond anyone's wildest dreams. Anyone can install this implant, and they won't even need to work to succeed at their exams. Do you have any idea of what candidates would be ready to pay for this?" A dark, amused smile. "But of course you wouldn't sell it, or even put it to use." The tile on the table shone: the upright scholar, the hollow bamboo without greed or worldly attachments, the perfect servant of the state, all probity and fairness… "It's just wasted on you. You'll hardly notice that it's gone."

In Vân's thoughts, An Thành was quoting *The Tale of Kiều* on bitter upheavals: *mulberry fields stretching into vast seas…*

Vân would notice. She would notice that her anchor and her comfort was gone—that An Thành was gone. She—

"Younger sister," Vân said, and this time she choked on the words, struggling to breathe. "Please…"

She'd expected Hương Lâm to laugh or gloat, but her friend's face was grave. "Just sleep." She rose from the table, leaving the teacup on its ruins. "I'll take what I need and be on my way. You'll wake up and be back to your old life soon."

Vân's head lay against the back of the chair, arms and legs flopping. Even thinking about moving was a struggle against the darkness pressing against her. She tried to say "elder sister", found only oppressive silence in her mouth.

Please. Please don't take her.

"Ssh," Hương Lâm said, and laid a hand, almost gently, on Vân's lips. "Sleep. It's almost over." And then the room dilated and unfocused—and Vân was trying to hold onto An Thành, to keep her always with her—*don't leave me please don't leave me*—but her eyelids were too heavy, and the world slid and fuzzed away from her.

"HMM," *SUNLESS WOODS* said. She was outside the place Thiên Hoa had indicated: a rundown compartment in a rundown area of the habitat, with a faint sheen on its bulging door—the metal had probably been scavenged from a mindship, which was an incongruous sight in an area this poor.

No one appeared to be about, but there was a pad with a code by the door's side.

"I could probably knock it down," Thiên Hoa said, chewing on a betel sweet. Her bots were shining like rings on her fingers. "Or hack it, but it would take some time. It's really one of the newfangled things, isn't it? Someone has been busy kitting themselves out." She sounded grudgingly admiring.

Sunless Woods was all grudges, and no admiration. "I don't have time for any of this." She still knew how long, to the blink, hacking the pad would require as a bare minimum. But there were other, less legal ways: all the things she'd learned in the faraway time when she'd fought in the empire's wars. She put in a query to the habitat's Mind, signaling a life-threatening emergency that would require the use of a disabling pulse.

Thiên Hoa, who was a co-recipient of the query, grimaced. "That's not subtle."

"Mm." *Sunless Woods* would have already sent the pulse, but doing so on a habitat loaded with bots and technology required precautions—she was quite likely to be arrested if she didn't at least make an effort to follow protocol. She was counting on this being a rundown neighbourhood, far away from the Mind's densest cloud of sensors or bots who could intervene—counting down, sexagen-mark by sexagen-mark, the time it took the Mind to reach a decision.

Any time now.

Any time…

"You are cleared for use over the following zone," the habitat's Mind said. She didn't sound overly happy. "You will file in a substantiated report, and commit to compensating for any personal damages to bots, overlay projectors and other technological items, if it is deemed necessary."

Which was likely to be interesting, but a problem for another time. *Yes, Sunless Woods* said, and directed her more heavy-duty bots to crawl over the door and its frame.

Now.

Even with heavier bots, the not entirely legal kind, and for ships rather than people, it was a weak pulse: focused rather than wide-range, a blast that tore through the door and everything in the building—weakening fast, but since all buildings were narrow, it meant any bots in there would now be fried. Thiên Hoa detached herself from the wall just as the bots pushed the door away from its frame. It creaked, with a screech like an arc-cutter on metal. Her smile was wide and wicked, exactly like old times, as she finished the bots' work by kicking the door down, *Sunless Woods* on her heels.

In the darkened corridor behind them, *Sunless Woods* kept a wary eye for muscle, but there was nothing in Thiên Hoa's wake—no one, not bots, not a single movement.

At the exit of the corridor, the room widened into the remnants of a teahouse, the kind that was a gambling den or a drug house or both. A single table remained in the centre, and the overlay, its projectors weakened by the pulse, flickered and expanded and twisted, throwing incoherent images of dragons and flowers and Heaven knew what across the darkened walls. Dead bots crunched under Thiên Hoa's feet.

"You're making quite an arrival." The woman was waiting for them by a door to the right, arms crossed over her chest. Her bots hung, limp, in the tangle of her hair. Behind her was another, burlier person, warily eyeing Thiên Hoa, who merely grinned, pointing to her own live bots, making it clear that she might be smaller and less strong but she'd win the fight anyway.

"Lê Thị Hương Lâm, I presume." *Sunless Woods* put the cutting edge of diamond blades in her voice.

A snort. "I have no idea who you are, but you're inconvenient. You're interrupting something."

Sunless Woods shifted, stretching her avatar so that it would show the stars and the habitats and the cold light of the sun, towering over the slight build of Hương Lâm. "I'm the person who's going to have a talk with you. As an alternative to other worse things."

Hương Lâm's face didn't move—almost, but her eyes did, and *Sunless Woods* saw it: she was rattled. Not necessarily cowed, but uncertain and thrown off-balance.

Good enough.

"Talk," Hương Lâm said.

The overlay flickered over her, showing fragments of calligraphied characters.

"Most of your accomplices are gone," *Sunless Woods* said. "You've stretched yourself very, very thin. And for sure you're not seeing again the bots you're scrabbling to bring back online. They're dead."

"I can replace them. Money can be found."

"Can it? You're desperate. You gambled everything on Ngân Chi's treasure, and panicked when it turned out to be a mirage. And—" *Sunless Woods* checked on her bots' feedback—"you've got a couple days, maybe less, before the exile implants kill you. And if you think it's hard now to withstand the pain, it'll get worse. Much much worse. But then you know this, because someone already died on your watch."

"Don't talk of Dinh."

Sunless Woods smiled, making it every bit inhuman and unsettling: her mouth a gaping maw of darkness, her teeth gleaming in the fragment of calligraphied words from the broken overlay, her face utterly still and wrongly proportioned. She shifted, slightly, and when she spoke again it was with the accent of a much lower social class than scholars. "Of course I'll talk of Dinh. Aren't elder sisters meant to protect their young ones? Heads of bands take care of their own?"

Hương Lâm's face was a rictus. "This isn't my failure."

"Oh, convenient excuses. All of it is your failure. Wanting out of exile isn't all bad, but you've spectacularly bungled it by all metrics. Your plan's in tatters. You killed your crew. And the militia has Ái Hồng's body. They may not be adding Dinh's death to your offences. But we both know the truth. Oh, I forgot the part where you're dying by bits from something worse than the slow death."

She could see Hương Lâm's vitals: measure every nuance of her heartbeat and skin temperature, the elevation from already high levels of pain to high levels of stress. She didn't care. Hương Lâm had earned every bit of what was coming to her.

At length Hương Lâm said, "You're not here to gloat."

"I'm here because I'm not amused," *Sunless Woods* said, sharply. "This is my home, and there won't be tantrums here, you snotty-faced larva."

Hương Lâm's mouth opened, like a fish gasping for air. *Sunless Woods* didn't leave her time to speak.

"A good thing you have been unsubtle and blundering through your blood-soaked failures." She was seeing, again and again, the body of Dinh, splayed on the overlay of stars and poetry in Uyên's bedroom; the body of Ái Hồng in the sterile chamber, the sad, hollow thing that had been a human being, taken apart by bots like a puzzle to be unlocked. "The militia won't need much help for a conviction. And you're a relapse. They'll probably not even wait for the Autumn Assizes. Or better yet, let you die from the breached exile while the Empress deliberates on whether you deserve the death penalty. A question we both know the answer to, but you might well expire in agony before she officially answers it."

"They wouldn't." Hương Lâm's face was white, leeched of all colours in the kaleidoscope of the broken overlay.

Sunless Woods smiled again, dropped into scholar's formality again. "What a delightful hope."

When Hương Lâm spoke, it was with a visible effort; her face contracted into pain or fear or both. Good. "*You* wouldn't."

"Wouldn't I? As I said—my home, my territory, my rules. Don't you dare soil it all."

A silence. Then Hương Lâm said, again, "You haven't come here to gloat. What do you want?"

VÂN WOKE UP to an insistent, high-pitched keening in her ears. She rolled over, raising hands that felt like jelly to cover them, but it made no difference, the sound wouldn't stop or let up—and then she realised it wasn't a sound, but Ai Tran's voice, rapidly repeating words that Vân couldn't make out—what—why—what was happening?

It was a saying from Master Khổng, repeated over and over at such a high speed the words blurred into each other, but then everything lurched and slowed down as Vân rolled over and vomited the entire contents of her stomach on some pristine metal floor, heaving again and again until only nauseating bile came up.

A gentleperson sees righteousness, an inferior one only advantage. A gentleperson sees righteousness, an inferior one only advantage. A gentleperson sees righteousness...

An Thành! I'm awake.

A gentleperson... An Thành's voice slowed down, gradually, as Vân's own thought processes settled back into place—and then she remembered the stomach-clenching fear with which she'd gone to sleep. What—

Hương Lâm. She'd wanted to take An Thành from her. She—

I am here, An Thành said. And, softly, *not leaving you*—repeating Vân's last incoherent thoughts, which she'd interpreted as a need for her to provide guidance—to keep Vân awake at all costs with whatever means she had at hand.

Vân forced herself to breathe until the frantic beating of her heart slowed down, until it no longer felt that every beat echoed in her chest and in her arms. *Not leaving you*, she said, not quite believing in the words herself.

She lay on a metal surface: an operating table, except that the restraints at head, wrists, ankles, legs and chest were open, and unresponsive bots lay scattered on the floor, along with broken medical equipment. She rolled off the table—it took an effort of will to do so, because she was shaking like a leaf, and she couldn't quite shake that nauseous feeling at the back of her throat. What had happened?

The mental equivalent of a shrug from An Thành. Of course she'd have been knocked into unconsciousness at the same time as Vân, even if she'd returned to operational a fraction of a second before Vân came back to full wakefulness.

But then An Thành said, thoughtfully, *Poisoned tea was good to knock you out, but not enough for an operation that amounts to opening your skull and doing fine manipulations on your brain. The bots were meant to inject you with other products.*

And something had interrupted them. Something which had also kept Hương Lâm from being in the room. Vân rubbed her wrists, trying not to think of her head split open like a fruit. She felt slight reddened marks where the bots had put on the restraints too fast. For all of Hương Lâm's professions of not wanting to harm her, she wouldn't much have cared about Vân's discomfort.

She didn't care, full stop. The thought was lodged like an iced rock in Vân's belly: that her friend had survived, but their friendship had not.

And was it all Hương Lâm's fault, in the end? Vân had chosen to remain silent; to live on stolen time, on wealth gained on her friends' punishment—and what did that make of her? A thief. A party to Dinh's death, as surely as Hương Lâm. A murderer.

Vân pulled herself up, shaking. Fell again, sprawling on the floor with her treacherous legs splayed in the corpses of bots—tried again and, finding no strength, crawled over to the operating table and used its edge to stand against, gripping it until the wave of dizziness had passed.

A gentleperson sees righteousness... An Thành was saying, gently, slowly, the same words she'd been screaming at her when Vân woke. *An inferior person sees only advantage.* And where was Vân's righteousness now—where it had ever been, when she'd betrayed her friends?

Vân managed, through trembling steps, to reach the wall or rather collapse against it, breath burning in her lungs. Righteousness. Advantage. She could hardly hear An Thành's voice, but she could feel her presence—a promise that she was here, that nothing would leave Vân feeling scared and vulnerable again.

Vân, choking on guilt, wasn't sure if she believed in that promise anymore.

She pushed herself forward, clinging to the wall—one step, two steps, collapsing against metal, and then pulling herself together again for another couple of steps, painstakingly making her way out of the room.

In the corridor were distant noises: Hương Lâm's, and another one, louder and brasher and almost familiar. As she got closer she finally recognised it: *Sunless Woods*.

I've never left someone in danger, and certainly not those I love.

You make it sound so simple.

That's because it is.

She'd come. She'd come for Vân. She—something was fluttering in Vân's chest, a trembling hope, an unfamiliar warmth—that she'd been seen, that she'd been judged, that she'd still been found worthy.

She'd come.

Vân pulled herself up, with renewed strength, and walked towards *Sunless Woods*.

IN THE TEAHOUSE, *Sunless Woods* faced Hương Lâm. A ping, on her comms: it was Uyên, who said she needed *Sunless Woods*'s opinion on something important. *Not now, Sunless Woods* said, annoyed, and buried the message at the bottom of her priority queue.

"What do I want?" she said. She let the question hang, while Thiên Hoa grinned at the last member of the band. "Fair things, really. A…" she rolled the word, letting it unfold in the air like a banner—"a toll."

"A toll." Hương Lâm's voice was flat.

"Oh, don't try that on me." She was going to try and dodge out of it, pretend that there'd never been any treasure of Ngân Chi. "We had a chat with Khê. We know about the other theft."

"The stuff of legend." Thiên Hoa's voice was flat, too; her face hard.

Hương Lâm stared at her, for a while. Something shifted in her stance. For some reason, *Sunless Woods* was losing her, and she didn't like this one bit. "That treasure isn't yours. You'll leave it to us, and then you'll leave."

"Back to my backwater planet?" Hương Lâm's voice was soft.

"I don't care where you go," *Sunless Woods* said, disquieted. "Just not here anymore."

Silence. Then Hương Lâm laughed. It was high-pitched and unpleasant, and on the verge of breaking apart, as if at any moment she was going to tear off a mask and reveal only malice. "Treasure," she said, sharply. "You're *thieves*."

"No shame in that," Thiên Hoa said.

Hương Lâm laughed again. "Thieves. Lecturing me on blood spilling and the soiling of your homes, but that's not what you dream of, isn't it? Just the money and the fame." Behind her came a small, soft noise like a piece of metal shaken loose: she turned, briefly, to face the darkness behind her. Whatever she saw, it caught her whole attention—she was lunging towards it before Thiên Hoa could even move, dragging something large and dark from the corridor behind her and throwing it at her feet, between *Sunless Woods* and her. "Well, there's your treasure beyond imagination, *thief.* Why don't you just take it all?"

And, as her laughter rose again, *Sunless Woods* saw, clearly, that the dark bundle in the centre wasn't an object, but a person. It was Vân.

FOR A LONG, agonising moment *Sunless Woods* could see nothing but Vân. Her hair was dishevelled—as she had been when they'd slept together, except that it was now matted with grease, and that she was as pale as rice paper, and shaking, huddling together as if she could make herself smaller.

She shouldn't have been there. She was safe. She—

Sunless Woods queried *Wine*—found her friend absorbed in her own work, reassuring her that no one had entered the house.

"Are you sure?" A fraction of a heartbeat, as *Wine* understood why *Sunless Woods* was asking, and the sharp, rising fear as they both realised what had happened.

No one had entered, but Vân had left.

The how or why of it could wait—there was an urgent situation to solve. *Find Uyên, Sunless Woods* said, remembering the call she hadn't had time to take. It was no longer on hold, and she had a sinking feeling Uyên had taken matters into her own hands.

Why could no one—except *Wine*—have the grace to stay in the safe places instead of blindly rushing into mortal danger?

"Thief," Vân whispered. She wasn't looking at *Sunless Woods*.

Thiên Hoa said, "She's not worth any money," a split second before *Sunless Woods* sent her a message to shut up.

"Her implant is." Hương Lâm hadn't moved, but she had an arc gun, and it was aimed at Vân's head. *Sunless Woods*'s reflexes were excellent, but a blink was all it'd take for Hương Lâm to fire.

Impasse.

Hương Lâm said, "You don't know what she made, do you? You weren't there to see it all happen. She didn't have scholar ancestors, so she invented herself one, six years ago. Scavenged other people's dead relatives for fragments and patterns."

She—*Sunless Woods* remembered Vân's diffidence, her utter conviction that her secret would lose her *Sunless Woods*'s regard. And no wonder. Using fake implants to gain a position was a scandal of such proportions. But there would be people willing to risk it, if it meant a chance to succeed at the examinations. If Vân was willing to sell. Which plainly, she hadn't been.

"Thief," Vân said, again. "You're a thief. You—" a deep, shuddering breath. "You came for me."

It was said with desolate intensity, and something stuttered and broke in *Sunless Woods*, as if someone had grabbed her faraway core and squeezed until everything flashed dark. *Lil'sis…*

How had she made such a mess of things?

A subvocalised ping from Thiên Hoa. *Focus. Because if you don't, there's only one way this ends, and it's going to be nasty all the way for your flirt.*

She's not—*Sunless Woods* started, and then stopped because it was pointless and just wasted time, and all she could see was the taut fear in Vân's eyes.

What mattered now wasn't what Vân thought about her—that gaping hole in her thoughts was a worry for another time—but saving Vân's life.

And that, in turn, meant making Hương Lâm believe she didn't care. Because she'd gain nothing by admitting to Hương Lâm she had *Sunless Woods*'s vulnerability within gun range.

She forced herself to be quiet; to lean forward with the familiar drawl in her mouth, the one that masked how angry she was: "You're mistaken. I don't take messed-up leftovers." And looked away from Vân, so that she wouldn't see the pain in Vân's face—and how much further her words shattered every fragile hope they'd ever had of building something together.

UYÊN HAD A plan, and it was all going downhill—first and foremost because *Wine* was throwing as many obstacles in her path as she could. Uyên had enough aunts of her own, and didn't need an extra one thinking she needed to be coddled like a fragile flower.

"I disagree," the ship was saying.

Uyên sent minute adjustments to the burden her bots were carrying for her. "I would be very glad to hear in what specific way." She didn't break stride, or do more than cursorily stare at *Wine*.

"*Sunless Woods* has the matter well under control."

The ship's voice projected far too much confidence: that meant either the problem was non-existent, or—more likely— it was going very, very badly and she didn't want Uyên to panic.

Which Uyên wasn't going to do, as that would have been the height of unconstructive. She still hadn't forgiven the ship for explaining the precise nature of the danger faced by her teacher three full centidays after said teacher had vanished, far too late for Uyên to try and set anything into motion. And *Sunless Woods*…let's just say Uyên gave *Sunless Woods* the bene- fit of the doubt only because Vân had sounded so happy when speaking of her. "If she has everything sorted out, surely my showing up won't do anything other than embarrass me. And I'm still young enough that I don't mind." The risk of a loss of face against the risk to Vân's life…that wasn't really a dilemma worth more than a blink's thought.

A silence. Uyên said, "It's gone wrong, hasn't it? Do you just intend to hover by and watch? That's going to get her killed."

She wanted to be near Vân so badly—to snatch her before anyone had a chance to harm her—and if *Wine* had been physically manifested, she'd have tried to grab and shake the ship regardless of their size difference. "Where is she? Exactly." Second Mother's friend at the tribunal had used not entirely legal means to track Vân to the Six Families district, but that wasn't precise enough.

Wine said, stiffly, "You cannot possibly intend to walk into danger."

Uyên—the daughter of the Captain who Swam in the River of Stars, the officer who had cold-bloodedly given her life to stop the Rợ—rolled her eyes to the Heavens, and laughed. "Watch me."

A GAPING HOLLOW had opened in Vân's belly, sucking all the warmth from her.

Sunless Woods was a thief.

She'd been hiding something—of course they'd both been hiding something, of course they'd understood what they'd shared was sex and not intimacy, of course Vân had known there was more to *Sunless Woods*, mild quirks, small chips in the cold and perfect smoothness of jade.

It was not small, or mild, or anything easily set aside.

She'd cared. She'd come back. She—

Every one of these halting thoughts shattered themselves against the cold wall of *Sunless Woods*'s anger: the ship was leaning forward, her whole body angled as though she was about to ram both Vân and Hương Lâm and didn't much care who she harmed. Her voice, when she spoke again, was that freezing coldness Vân had heard in the corridor, the same contemptuous, mocking tone that had stopped Vân in her trembling advance towards what she'd naively believed freedom—until she realised that, like any good thieves, Hương Lâm and *Sunless Woods* were arguing about how best to share the loot before the militia arrived.

And the loot was her.

She'd sent *Wine*. She'd come—she—

But all she'd come for was gain; and the only reason she'd sent *Wine* instead of herself was so she'd have a better chance at beating Hương Lâm to the wealth. And she might not have expected such wealth to be walking and talking—

Not quite, An Thành said, drily. *I don't exactly walk. You do that part.*

You're missing the point!! Vân snapped. *You just don't*—she stopped, then, because she couldn't be sure of what An Thành did and didn't understand.

You're upset. Inability to calm the mind hinders the path to tranquility and awakening.

As if that helped.

Far, far away, Hương Lâm was saying, "Bedraggled? You're unfair. She's cleaned up quite well, considering."

As if Vân weren't even there. But she didn't even have the strength to stand up anymore.

Sunless Woods didn't even flinch. "I'm a thief, not a murderer."

"I wasn't suggesting a murder." Hương Lâm's voice was equable. "Merely a quick and dirty extraction with an equal share of the proceeds between us. A comfortable stash to sit on."

"An extraction which she likely wouldn't survive," *Sunless Woods*'s companion said.

"I don't take people apart for gain." *Sunless Woods* stretched—and as she did the floor under her became studded with darkness, the fragments of mạt chược tiles barely containing the coat of heavenly stars spreading out from her—and she was terrible and beautiful, and as uncaring as the void that choked, burning as bright as comets' tails, turning the breath in Vân's lungs into searing emptiness. "And neither will you, not while I'm here."

She'd come, and she didn't care one jot.

A sharp laugh from Hương Lâm. "Principles. You're not desperate enough, are you." A rustle of cloth—someone shouting, and the sharp noise of bots moving, and then the cold of Hương Lâm's gun was against Vân's chest, in the hollow of her collarbone.

"Don't," she said, matter-of-factly. "I'll kill her if the bots get any closer."

IT HAD BEEN a bad and desperate plan, made in the heat of the moment and with not much ground on which to negotiate. Make Hương Lâm realise that Vân was of no value to her because *Sunless Woods* wouldn't let Hương Lâm take the implants—a dangerous gamble that Hương Lâm still had a conscience and wouldn't kill her former friend.

Very, very dangerous, and not working at all.

It had been her failure in the first place, her sheer bone-headedness that had led to Vân being there, struggling to rise—no, she wasn't even struggling anymore, she'd slumped to the ground and wasn't moving, and Hương Lâm's gun rested against her chest, and everything was infinitely worse than it had been moments ago.

Sunless Woods had pulled herself out of worse scrapes—had snatched Hải's children from the execution field moments before the noose closed over their necks, grabbed the Emperor's drinking cups as the guard hammered against the door and *Wine* gibbered about the punishment that awaited them. She couldn't possibly be failing. She couldn't possibly be outsmarted by an exiled thief and her muscle. She couldn't possibly have lost her touch so badly.

She—

HƯƠNG LÂM'S HAND as she held the gun didn't tremble. She said, in a voice so low that *Sunless Woods* wouldn't hear her,

"You know this was always coming to this. Full circle to us. I would have died for you, five years ago. I remained silent and out of your life until I couldn't bear it anymore. But now it's time. Give me the mem-implant."

"I can't," Vân whispered.

"Because you're afraid? You've always understood duty, big'sis. Do you not understand where it leads?" And, in a softer voice, "If we hadn't remained silent, you wouldn't be there. You wouldn't have your quiet, guiltless life."

Because she had failed them. Because she had failed all of them as she was failing at her life—letting Hương Lâm and Dinh protect her, not understanding who *Sunless Woods* really was. Because, in the end, even An Thành was an illusory comfort, one that couldn't disguise the truth of who Vân was: a coward who'd tried to run away from the weight of her faults—who prided herself on her honesty and was really not worth anything more than Hương Lâm. A deluded sinner who'd let Hương Lâm and Dinh suffer, who'd stood by while Dinh died.

"Tell her," Hương Lâm said. "Tell her you're giving up the mem-implant of your own free will."

"Lil'sis—"

"Tell her, or you'll die."

Vân opened her mouth—and wasn't even sure of what she'd said—when a high-priority message blinked in her inbox. Before she could even think of dismissing it, it opened up like a flower, and she heard Uyên's voice.

"Teacher?"

It was Uyên's voice, coming from infinitely far away.

"Teacher?"

"Not now."

"Teacher, where are you? I'm coming."

"You can't possibly—"

When Uyên spoke again, her voice had changed: no longer panicked or frightened, but deeper and sharper. "Of course I can. Tell me where you are, and hang on. I'm not far away."

"I—" But An Thành was already sending it through, a bright, shining dot on their position.

Never leave me, she said, simply. And, in a lower voice, a quote that didn't sound from any of the Classics: *I can make the fear go away, if you'll let me. Let me care*—until Vân realised that An Thành was merely quoting *Sunless Woods's* words to her, moments before they'd slept together.

Uyên's voice still echoed in Vân's thoughts. *I'm coming.*

Vân stared at the gun, feeling its coldness against her chest. A primal, pared-down thought rose in her: she was Uyên's teacher, and she couldn't allow her student to find her like this.

"No," she said. And laid both hands on the gun, pushing it away from her—Hương Lâm, shocked, barely offered any opposition—her finger reflexively pushed the trigger, and the shot, whizzing past Vân's ears, buried itself in the floor. A distant scream that had to be *Sunless Woods,* high-pitched and inhuman. Had—had she just been faking it all, the nonchalance just a façade?

Vân couldn't afford the distraction of dwelling on this.

"No," Vân said, again. It took all her strength to maintain her hold—to keep the gun pointed away from her, while Hương Lâm tried to bring it back where it had been, on the edge of going through Vân as easily as through wet rice paper. Her hands shook from the effort—behind her, another scuffle, but everything she was boiled down to this single gesture, this single effort of holding Hương Lâm at bay.

"Ingrate," Hương Lâm hissed. Her face—her unfamiliar, alien face—was twisted in pain. "You can't mean to leave it all meaningless. To have it all come to nothing."

Sunless Woods's scream echoed in Vân's thoughts, over and over: that sharp and endless shock, as if she could have held the bullet back. A fragile, breathless hope balanced with anger—if she did care, how dare she let Vân think otherwise?

"Let her go." It was Uyên's voice, and it rang under the ceiling like a call of the names in the Pavilions of the Meritorious. "Now."

Hương Lâm laughed. "You really think—" And then she stopped, and her hands stopped, too, and the gun, pushed only by Vân, clattered to the floor, ringing with the same clamour as if it had gone off.

Vân forced herself to move; crawled, bit by bit, to it, and curled around it, both hands wrapped around its handle so that no one could claim it.

Only then did she look up.

The woman with *Sunless Woods* had taken down Hương Lâm's accomplice, and her bots were holding her to the ground—which had to be both the scuffles she'd heard. *Sunless Woods* stood, motionless, with a widening overlay of stars around her, an oily sheen clinging to her hands between the fingers, and around her neck, descending to her shoulders— trembling, and her eyes filled with tears.

Hương Lâm, too, stood motionless. She was looking at Uyên. Or rather, at what Uyên was now holding in her hands.

It was Dinh's corpse.

She was naked, with the incision marks of the autopsy on her chest and wrists: she hung limply in Uyên's grasp, her greying hair streaming towards the floor, the colour of a stormy sky on the First Planet, her eyes open and unseeing, their whites now completely taken over by the grey tinge of the exile-implant's toxins—and discoloration all over her tanned skin, darker, bluer stains that made it all seem unreal. Behind Uyên was the smaller shape of *Wine*, the ship uncannily silent and still.

Uyên held Dinh out to Hương Lâm. The bots that had been helping her hold Dinh up scattered, the clicking of their legs resonating on the metal floor, but Uyên's arms barely sagged, and her face remained steely and cold. She said, simply, "It's an elder sister's duty to take care of a younger one."

Hương Lâm's face was pale, as bloodless as the corpse in Uyên's hands. "She chose to come here."

"And she died here." Uyên's bots were coming towards Hương Lâm: they held a pair of chopsticks, a few grains of rice, and three coins, the accoutrements of a dead body. "You'd have taken the money, and left her to become a hungry ghost with no relative to claim her?"

Hương Lâm's face was taut, and Vân couldn't tell anymore what was pain from the exile implants and what was sheer grief. "She'd have understood."

"Ghosts seldom do, do they? Ask all the reanimated un-mourned spirits if they understand why they feed on the living." Uyên's voice was soft. "Take her and leave."

Hương Lâm said, "This isn't over." But the certainty in her voice was gone.

"You know it is. Take her. Send her on, to the proper court of hell. Send her on to be reincarnated. Do your duty."

"Duty." Hương Lâm's voice was bitter. "Not something I've ever been much for."

Uyên said nothing. She simply stood, holding Dinh's body: her face set, her entire stance making her seem larger than she was, a fact of life that wouldn't be moved or ignored—and in that moment Vân saw clearly the official she'd become, the hollow bamboo arcing straight towards its goal, unswayed by temptation or worldly attachments—her student, the teenager she'd taught become adult, and pride swelled in her chest like a huge bird spreading wings.

When Hương Lâm moved, it was slow and tentative, and in utter silence. She walked like a puppet moved by a distant master, limbs jerking in a subtly off way, too fast, too disconnected. Her hands closed around Dinh's body, her face that of a person dying of thirst and offered water—her mouth shaping soundless words—*a prayer*, An Thành said, unnecessarily. Hương Lâm closed her eyes, too, briefly, when the weight shifted and the body rested in her arms—and she shifted it over her shoulder, head lolling downwards. In that same unnatural stillness, she walked towards the exit to the room, no one making a move to stop her.

She paused, once, looking at Vân: her eyes were shadowed and haunted, and in her gaze was that same heart-breaking expression Vân had seen five years ago, that same admonition to remain silent, to save herself. "It's my fault," she said, shaking her head. "It could have gone so many other ways, with so much less harm." Beneath her were the fragments of mạt chược tiles, the Seven of Threads, the Seven of Infinities, the Seven of Barrels. "Goodbye, big'sis. Remember me."

And then she was gone, and Vân was still curled around the gun, struggling to breathe.

UP TO THE last moment, *Sunless Woods* had expected it would turn out all right—that she'd rustle up a miracle, turn this on its head the way she always turned things around, that things were bleak and desperate but that she'd find a way. That she'd come out of this the way she always had, with a daring escape that let her be the darling of memorials and newscasts.

Until Vân grabbed the gun from Hương Lâm, and *Sunless Woods*'s entire world narrowed to that silent struggle—and the detonation, and her whole consciousness focused into that single, primal scream that tore from her distant core all the way into the habitat—and then Uyên walking in and effortlessly managing the situation while *Sunless Woods* stood frozen, seeing, over and over, the shot so close to Vân's face, how close she'd come to losing it all.

Because of her single focus and arrogance, and mistaken belief she could do it all, because she thought she could show off and save Vân, and still find a way to salvage it all.

Because of her.

She should be moving now. She should be taking charge, making sure that Vân was safe, that things resolved the way they should. Thiên Hoa was staring at her, wondering why she wasn't—why Uyên, barely old enough to be considered out of childhood, was the one who seemed to be in charge.

Sunless Woods just stood there, trying to patch together her shattered thoughts.

"TEACHER, TEACHER." IT was Uyên's voice, and her student's hands, gently uncurling her. "Come on come on, Teacher."

Vân tried to rise, found only shaking in her arms and legs. Uyên was pressing something in her hands, and then into her mouth when it didn't work. A short burst of rich sweetness in her mouth: it was some kind of flaky durian cake, a thin outer layer that melted, leaving only the savour of the fruit.

"She needs a doctor," *Sunless Woods*'s companion was saying.

Uyên's voice was savage. "Don't even think of interfering in this. You've done enough as it is." *Sunless Woods* still hadn't moved: or more accurately she'd relaxed but was still staring at Vân with tears streaming down in her face. Good, because Vân wasn't sure of what she'd have told her.

An Thành said, sharply, *She lied, earlier. When she referred to you as messed-up leftovers.*

Why would she? But she knew, didn't she. Because if she'd told Hương Lâm how much she cared, Hương Lâm would have held Vân hostage.

Understanding didn't make Vân less angry, or bereft. *She had no right.*

From An Thành, only silence.

"Better?" Uyên asked. "Teacher?"

The statesperson's pose was gone, and now she looked as though she'd crossed ten courts of Hell to get there.

"I'm all right." Vân tried to pull herself upwards again—managed it finally, shaking, on legs that still felt like jelly. "Thank you."

Uyên's smile was dazzling. "That was only the right thing to do."

Remember me, Hương Lâm had said, before walking away—before once more leaving Vân to carry on with her life. Duty. Truth. Integrity. All the hidden things, and the lie she'd built for herself, and the past that she couldn't escape. How could she pretend to be a teacher, if she wasn't telling Uyên who helped her provide the teachings? "Child," she said. "There's something you need to know. About me. About my honored ancestor." She braced herself then, feeling An Thành in her thoughts, the leaden weight that would crush the life she'd built. But it was the right thing to do. "A long time ago, I—"

Uyên's finger rested on her mouth, lightly—but as rigid as a bar of steel. "I don't need to know."

"But—" Vân started. That wasn't what she'd expected.

Uyên's face was grave. "We are what we are. What we made ourselves into. The choices we made. I've seen it, Teacher. That's all that matters."

"I've done things you wouldn't forgive."

Uyên cocked her head. "Ah. We all do these, don't we?"

Vân thought of the gun, and the utter certainty that she couldn't let Uyên see her that way—that she needed to stand up and live. "I'm your teacher."

Laughter. "You say that like you should be perfect. Trust me, Teacher, you don't need to be."

"You can't mean—"

"To forgive you? I already have." Uyên smiled, and once again it felt as though the whole room, ramshackle overlay and all, was flooded with light. She laughed. "After all, I've just helped a murderer escape justice. I can't even say I have a very firm grounding on keeping with the law."

I've done things you wouldn't forgive.

We all do these, don't we?

She had failed her friends. She had been dishonest and cowardly, and nothing would change that. She thought of *Sunless Woods*, of An Thành; of Uyên and of Hương Lâm, walking away from her.

She couldn't escape her past, but she could acknowledge it—could own it, let it be part of who she was rather than having it destroy her. She could know who she was, and forgive herself. "The militia—"

"Oh, don't worry about that. I'll deal with the militia. Or *Sunless Woods* will."

Sunless Woods. Thief. Her mocking words, echoing in Vân's thoughts, again and again, the easy lies, the arrogance. But she was standing stock-still and still hadn't moved, and her scream still echoed in Vân's thoughts, and Vân didn't know, anymore, what to do.

Uyên's face shifted. "I see," she said. "Come on."

⁝
○

IN THE END, it was Uyên and Vân who came to her: Vân shaking and in obvious shock, and Uyên's gaze dark and piercing, decidedly unfriendly, as if at any moment she would lecture *Sunless Woods* heedless of their age difference.

"Thank you," *Sunless Woods* said. "For what you did."

An expansive shrug, from Uyên. "Only the righteous thing." Her eyes glinted. "Sorting out the situation with the militia should be interesting."

Behind them, Thiên Hoa raised a suggestive eyebrow. Time to show off; to impress Vân—except that she'd almost gotten Vân killed, and had hurt her prior to that. She should leave— run and change her identity, the way she always had. She'd tried to bring changes in her life, and nothing had worked out. Time to start over with her crew, find fresh wrongs to be righted, or valuables to be stolen.

"I don't know who you are," Uyên said.

"Not a scholar," Vân whispered. And in her gaze was only anger and despair, an expression that shook *Sunless Woods* to her core.

She could run, again and again, trying to outpace her old life. Or she could try, for once, to go the hard way. She said, slowly, "Think of me as a help. I can work with the militia to finish untangling this, but the credit for all this is yours."

Uyên's gaze on her was ironic, and way too perceptive for a girl her age. "Thank you."

Vân's hand, resting on Uyên's. "Can I—"

Uyên's face softened. "Of course, Teacher." And stepped away, to leave the two of them some privacy.

"YOU WOULD HAVE let me die." Vân's voice was shaking. She couldn't seem to stand still—at length, she had to lean on the wall, struggling to breathe.

Sunless Woods said, finally, "No. I was trying very hard not to make that happen."

"You—you let me think I was *loot.*"

"I had to. I had to pretend I did not care, that I was as much of a thief as she was." The ship's voice was no longer as confident as it had once been. "By pretending you were worthless to her or me. It was the only way—"

"And look what happened! I—" a deep, shaking breath. "If I hadn't pushed her away…"

A silence. The ship wasn't looking at her. At length she said, and her voice was different, "It was a risk, and I should never have taken it. I'm sorry."

"I don't want your excuses." Vân tried to keep the bitterness from her voice, but it was hard. She understood why *Sunless Woods* had done it—she should have forgiven, but she just couldn't. It was too much.

"Are you going to reproach me for keeping secrets?"

"No," Vân said. "We both did that, and we knew it. I didn't take you into my confidence: I wasn't expecting to be taken into yours." She paused, then, because she didn't know what to expect anymore. And then, finally, "You lie with such ease. How can I ever be sure anything is the truth? How can I—" she stopped, then. "How can I even know if you cared at all?"

A silence. A gentle, trembling heat on her hands: *Sunless Woods*, wrapping her own hands around hers, her skin the colour of the night sky, with stars slowly winking on her fingers. "Because I do. Because I've never met anyone like you, and I let it blind me. Because I was thoughtless and arrogant." A deep, trembling breath from the ship: underneath them was the cloth of heaven, slowly spreading to Vân's feet and sheening with all the colours of the rainbow. "And because you're right. I can't make excuses that would atone for any of this. I just—" she withdrew her hands, gently reached up to tilt Vân's head up, to look into her deep, black gaze—"I just wanted you to know there's more to life than duty. That you've earned everything you have, and no life should ever become a chokehold or a cage. But that's arrogance too, isn't it, to hope that I can interfere in what's yours." An expressive shrug. "Take what you want from what we had. I just hope you'll remember it without regret."

"You're leaving," Vân said.

The ship shook her head. "No. I'm sticking around to see if Uyên needs help with the aftermath of any of this. But you don't have to deal with me. I'll talk to Uyên directly. You can go back to your old life."

Her old life. It should have felt like a relief, but the thought of it—of teaching Uyên, of being on the margins of society, barely tolerated—of having nothing but duty and obligations, with An Thành as her only comfort—was a leaden weight in her chest.

I don't want to go higher. I'm happy here, she had told Hương Lâm, and it had all felt like a lie, because it was one. Because she didn't want to become an official or rule, but there were other ways to reach out, to stretch past the boundaries she'd put on her own life.

She thought of the asteroid field and of the ship—of hanging weightless and without obligations, of what it had felt like to be free.

She'd forgiven herself—why should she not forgive *Sunless Woods?*

Sunless Woods said, "If I thought there was a chance, any chance that you'd leave it all behind for my sake, I'd ask." The ship's laughter was bitter. "But it would be unfair. Because I can't ordain your life as I see fit, or protect you from harm. In the end, the decisions are yours." She let go of Vân, and stood for a while, staring at her with that odd expression on her face.

And then she was turning away, gliding rather than walking, the darkness of the stars withdrawing from Vân, that trembling oily sheen travelling across her bare feet, An Thành silent and shocked in her mind as it all left—and she'd never felt so cold or so miserable or so small.

No life should ever become a chokehold or a cage.

"Big'sis," she said—and, as she'd once said while on the ship's body, "Wait. Please."

Sunless Woods paused; turned, watching her, with painful hope in her face. Vân said, haltingly, "I can't leave. I'm Uyên's teacher: I have obligations here. It just can't work that way."

"I see." The ship's voice was taut, braced for a blow.

Vân plunged on, "But we could find other ways to make it work."

A slow, heavy silence. *Sunless Woods* was by her side again; Vân had hardly seen her move; but felt her now, a dark, vast presence by her side, as inevitable and natural as the sun and the nebulae and the black holes. "You don't know what you're getting into," *Sunless Woods* said.

Vân smiled, then. "No. But neither do you. That's half the challenge, isn't it?"

And, gathering the strength she had left, she stood on tiptoe and kissed *Sunless Woods,* drinking in sheeny oil and sharp metal and the endless song of the stars—until *Sunless Woods* caught her in her arms, and she hung weightless and free, with nothing in the habitats holding her back anymore.

Acknowledgements

I WOULD LIKE to thank Tade Thompson, Marissa Lingen, Fran Wilde and Kate Elliott for beta-reading the draft of this book, and Hara Trần for double-checking all my Vietnamese names. For support, Stephanie Burgis, D Franklin, Zoe Johnson, Liz Bourke and Charlotte Cuffe, Elizabeth Bear, Scott Lynch, Adrian Tchaikovsky, Dev Agarwal, Zen Cho, Nene Ormes, Alessa Hinlo, Inksea, Sheila Perry, Stella Evans, Likhain, Juliet Kemp, Michelle Sagara, Samit Basu, Victor Fernando R Ocampo, Vida Cruz, Lynn E O'Connacht, Rachel Monte, Kari Sperring, Hana Lee, Ghislaine Lai, Justine, Nina Niskanen, Natasha Ngan, Liz Bourke, Laura J Mixon, Gareth L Powell, Cindy Pon, Alessa Hinlo, Rochita Loenen-Ruiz, Camille Regan, Jeannette Ng and Jenny Rae Rappaport.

Many thanks to Yanni Kuznia, Bill Schafer, Geralyn Lance, and everyone at Subterranean Press and Desert Isle Design for producing such a gorgeous book, and to Maurizio Manzieri for the gorgeous cover. To John Berlyne for advice and support, as always.

To my family for their support and love.

And to Maurice Leblanc and Arsène Lupin, for inspiring the character of *Sunless Woods* and her adventures!